Sherlock Holmes and The Case of the Edinburgh Haunting

David Wilson

Paperback ISBN 9781780922829
ePub ISBN 9781780922836
PDF ISBN 9781780922843

Published in the UK by MX Publishing
335 Princess Park Manor, Royal Drive, London, N11 3GX
www.mxpublishing.com

Cover design by www.staunch.com

Acknowledgement

I would like to thank Lynne Wilson for her support and excellent historical research which was invaluable in the writing of this book, as was her website

www.scotlandshistoryuncovered.com

PART 1

From the journal of Doctor John Watson

Chapter 1

The noise and bustle in Baker Street seemed to be of even greater notice to me the harder I tried to filter it out. The clatter of the hansoms trundling past or the young rascals causing mischief for the street vendors selling their food to the passers by, every small noise seemed to block out the one noise for which I was actually listening. That noise, although he would not thank me for describing it so, being my friend Sherlock Holmes and his infernal violin. It was this that was the very reason I had decided to take my Sunday constitutional before lunch rather than after, and was now trying to listen closely lest I return before it had been silenced. Not that my walk had been any less pleasant, watching my fellow Londoners out in their Sunday best returning from Church, making their way for lunch or to visit a relative in town. Since meeting Holmes and witnessing his singular gifts, I had tried to make time to study people as they went about their business and as far as I could tell there were some who would rather have been signed on at a tannery than spend the afternoon with their relatives. I wondered exactly what type of relatives they must have that would draw such a frown, and coming to the conclusion that it was perhaps better to at least have these relatives than to find oneself with none. However, you may not appreciate the former situation unless you were in the latter.

Being unable to detect any sound over the noise around me, and knowing that Mrs Hudson would be preparing a sumptuous lunch for us, I took my newspaper and my life in my hands and opened the front door and was immediately dismayed to hear the melancholy sound floating down the stairs. Mrs Hudson appeared from her scullery and took my hat and coat, "Doctor Watson, I am so glad you are back," she said, her manner unusually brusque, "Mr Holmes has been playing that musical instrument, for want of a better description, since you departed. I tried to serve him lunch but he would not have it and insisted we wait for your return." I smiled warmly at her,

"Very well Mrs Hudson, I'm here now. I suggest you serve lunch as quickly as possible." She bustled off in the direction of the kitchen out of my sight and the noise of dishes being hastily arranged onto a tray followed. I looked up to the landing willing my feet to follow which, to their credit, they most graciously agreed to do and I started to climb the stairs. I must admit to feeling somewhat churlish but for the last two days Holmes had been in a state of high energy with nothing on which to focus his attentions. His energy burst out from within him like the rays of the sun and it would surely take the magnifying glass of a case presenting itself to focus those rays onto a singular spot and draw his energy to a purposeful use. I opened the door to our parlour and saw Holmes standing in front of the window playing the violin while watching the people go by in the street.

"Holmes!" I shouted over the noise, "Holmes!" He stopped playing with a flourish of the bow and spun around to look at me, "I believe Mrs Hudson is bringing us lunch so perhaps we should sit down and be ready to receive?" He nodded his head and then stowed his violin on a chair before taking a seat at the table and gesturing me into the seat opposite.

"How was your walk today Watson?" he asked.

”Very satisfying, thank-you. Have you been playing since I left?”
“Indeed, Watson. I was caught up in the music and it helped to take my mind off my current idleness.” He glanced towards my newspaper lying folded on the table, “Is there any interesting news in today’s edition?” I gave him a wry smile,
“I know very well to what you are referring and yes there is a report on the event. Although to read it would scarcely beggar belief given that your name is yet again conspicuous by its absence while Lestrade and his men take the glory. I opened my paper to the relevant page and started to read a small section of the article, “*The Duke and Duchess of Connaught would like to thank the members of Scotland Yard who worked tirelessly to avert the tragedy. It is now well known in public circles that if the heinous plot to kidnap their young daughter on the day of her baptism had succeeded then it is believed a sizeable ransom would have been demanded for her safe return. The Duke and Duchess would like to thank the detectives for their tireless efforts as well as thanking the public for their many messages of support and good wishes.*” I closed the paper and put it down, “There, what do you make of that? Not even a word of thanks to you and I bet that Scotland Yard are quite happy to keep it that way.” Holmes laughed heartily,
“Quite right too, Watson. As I have said previously, nothing amuses me more than knowing that the Police are taking the credit for solving the crime yet, if they were asked any probing questions, they would show themselves to be utterly perplexed of how they came to solve the matter.” At that moment Mrs Hudson came into the room and placed lunch on

the table, with generous portions of roast beef, vegetables and gravy and then left without a word. Holmes still had a grin on his face and was lost in his own recollections which I could not understand,

"But does it not bother you that the Police are taking credit for your work?"

"Not one bit Watson. It is enough for me to know that Lestrade knows he did not solve it and I do not believe it will stop clients from seeking me out for further work. In truth the case itself was not a very complex one and the fears of the Duke and Duchess were overinflated in any case." He stopped to take a bite of his lunch, "Although it is possible that had my involvement not been assured by the Duke then events may have taken a turn for the worse and it would have been too late for me to resolve matters so successfully." He sat back and pondered this, "One thing I have learned, Watson, is that a job is twice as difficult when first requiring to correct the mistakes of the amateurs who have come before." I folded my paper and placed it back down on the table,

"Come now Holmes, I don't think it would be fair to label the police as amateurs. Lestrade and his men are known for doing some good work."

"True, I grant you that Watson. But if you require a table leg to be mended you may call for the services of a ha'penny joiner but the same tradesman would not do where a craftsman is required. I apply the same parallel to the capabilities of the police and to that of myself." He rose from the table and stood in front of the fire, filling his Cherry wood pipe with tobacco from the Persian slipper hanging on the mantle and then lighting up and drawing in deeply. I was glad

to see Holmes in such good spirits as he had for some time been in one of his morose states where he had seldom lifted his head or uttered a word. Prior to his engagement by the Duke of Connaught it had been some months since his previous case and he had fallen into a state of lethargy and despair the like of which I have never witnessed in another man. The case just completed had reinvigorated his spirits but I could see he was restless to be engaged in some other matter but thus far there was nothing to which he could apply his expertise. I lit a cigar and sat in my chair at the fire,
"What will you do while I'm away Holmes?" My trip to Edinburgh to visit my cousin, Patrick, had been planned for some weeks and it was made clear on several occasions that Holmes was welcome to accompany me. "You seem to be itching to be about something and if there is no case to work on then I believe you will take refuge in your old friend and slide back into your dark moods." He smiled slightly,
"My dear Watson," said he, "it is true that I do value your company and with nothing to occupy me then you shall be missed, but the idea of an eleven hour train journey does not fill me with a happy anticipation. You will of course give my apologies to your cousin?"
"Of course I will, although I know he was very much looking forward to meeting you. My train does not leave until this evening so there is time yet for you to reconsider, especially since the journey would give us ample opportunity to write up the notes on your last case." He gave me a hasty scornful glance,
"How you dramatise my work in your journal is of very little interest to me as you well know. I can barely content myself to read your accounts of my cases with all of the dramatic

liberties you take. The facts should be enough to speak for themselves, Watson."

"Yes, so you have said." I replied, sighing and rubbing my brow. I felt it was pointless to try to press him further when a small glint of hope presented itself in my mind. "I would have thought that a man such as you, Holmes, would relish a trip to Edinburgh to rub shoulders with the great and the good in the scientific world? The medical school is among the finest in the world and new progress is being made there constantly." He drew on his pipe and gazed at the fire but did not respond. "Surely you must wish to keep up with the latest discoveries to ensure your knowledge is at the cutting edge for your profession?" I asked. He blew out a billow of smoke and raised his eyebrows,

"I am well acquainted with the work in Edinburgh and see no reason to travel the length of the entire country for such a purpose since, for some time, I have taken a subscription to the Edinburgh Medical Journal which I find most informative."

"Aah," said I eagerly, "then you will be familiar with Dr. Joseph Bell who edits the Journal?"

"Indeed," he responded with another cloud of smoke punctuating his acknowledgement, "in fact I have read his Manual of the Operations of Surgery as part of my investigation into the intricacies of the human body. A more enjoyable and informative work I have yet to encounter, although I must admit Watson that I have made some minor notes in the margins." I watched him closely as he returned his gaze to the crackling fire.

"Did you know that Dr. Bell is a close colleague and friend of my cousin Patrick? I am sure you would find it even more informative if you were to meet him in person, which I am sure could be arranged. I understand from Patrick that Dr. Bell is most curious to meet you as he understands that you are using his methods in your chosen field." I continued to watch him closely and I would swear on oath that a wisp of a smile crossed his mouth and then vanished in a swirl of smoke as his glinting eyes darted towards me and then back to the fireplace,

"I am immune to your game Watson, you must know that. If Dr. Bell is under such a misunderstanding it is unfortunate but, having said that, I must admit to a modicum of curiosity to see how he is using *my* methods in the practice of medicine." He rose from his chair and returned to look out of the window again, looking both ways along Baker Street before turning back to face me again. "Since it seems that London can look after itself for the time being Watson, then I will accept the kind invitation of your cousin to avail myself of his hospitality in Edinburgh." He paused momentarily, "I can only hope it is not too little notice for him to make a room available for me given my late change of mind?" I stood up and walked towards the door,

"No need to worry Holmes," said I, "I will telegraph him at once to let him know you will be accompanying me after all." I smiled and darted out of the door but had gone no more than three paces when he shouted me back,

"Watson!" I returned and stood in the doorway, "You may think you are starting to know me too well my friend, however do not forget that I will always be one step ahead. There is no need to telegraph your cousin, Watson." I looked perplexed,

“Really, but why?” He gave me a withering look, although his eyes glinted mischievously,
“Because you have not telegraphed him in the first place to inform him I would not be coming!” said he forcefully.
“But…”
“Not another word, Watson,” he lowered his pipe and smiled curiously in my direction before turning back to the window again, “I shall be ready to leave at six thirty sharp! I trust you will arrange us a cab to the station.”

Chapter 2

Our journey to St. Pancras was made mostly in silence with Holmes only enquiring if I had brought my service revolver to which I confirmed in the positive. I had seldom carried it with me previously but since meeting Holmes I seldom had occasion to be without it. Not that I generally had any need to use it but the security of having it about my person was comforting. We arrived at the station just before seven o'clock and as I paid the cabbie, I observed Holmes standing facing the station entrance, watching the hordes of people going past. No-one was overlooked from his gaze, from the finest gentleman to the lowest beggar, the most beautiful lady to the foulest guttersnipe, all were worthy of the same attention from Holmes. I marvelled again at the fact that he should never miss an opportunity to carry out further study on his fellow man. I had remarked upon this once previously and he had retorted that 'a man can never allow himself to believe he knows everything Watson, or else he will find himself the most ignorant among men!' This was a feeling with which, being a man of medicine and education, I heartily agreed and it was with some satisfaction that I believed that our trip to Edinburgh would help to satisfy both our needs for enrichment.

Inside the cavernous terminal of St. Pancras I engaged a porter for our bags and we followed him through the throng of people to the platform for the overnight train to Edinburgh. It was a relief to cocoon ourselves in our compartment away from the bustle outside and after stowing our luggage we settled down into our seats. "We should be off at eight o'clock," said I, "then we can enjoy the last of the evening

light as we go." Holmes was gazing out of the window from the seat opposite and nodded only slightly at my remark,
"Quite so, Watson. I trust you have your notebooks with you in order that we can finalise your account of the Case of the Connaught Abduction?" I nodded, and waved the book in the air,
"Indeed I do, although I'm surprised you are so keen to help with it - I recollect that there was a certain sneering from some quarters in regard to my accounts of your cases?" I teased him.
"Not sneering Watson, I am interested merely to ensure the facts of the case are correct and documented accordingly. Now I believe we had reached the point at which the Duke of Connaught thanked me personally for my intervention?"
"We did…" I read aloud the last page or so that I had written in order that we could pick up the thread of our narrative and, despite his protestations to the contrary, the small satisfied smile on Holmes face suggested that he was not as averse to my writings as he would have me believe.
"Excellent, Watson, the meat of the facts are all there even if dressed up in your usual way. Now, let us continue."
As the train propelled its way out of London and through the green countryside, which was now made a darker shade by the dying light, I noted down Holmes' account of his deductions and reasoning of the case and was again in awe of his powers. The clues which had led him to his solution had been evident to me also, but I had not even guessed at the events that were to take place let alone in doing so prevent them from coming to their dreadful conclusion. To Holmes it almost seemed commonplace that he could see these, however that is the mark of a true craftsman, to make his

work look easy but the end result is far beyond the layman or less gifted in the field. Writing this account proved to be a useful activity with which to occupy us on the journey and by the time we had finished revising the notes we could no longer see anything through the windows other than our own reflections in the glass, the solid darkness covering all sight of the world outside. I closed my notebook and stretched my arms and back,

"Well, Holmes, I think I'll turn in now if you don't mind?"

Holmes nodded in agreement and we prepared our respective bunks in the compartment and then climbed in wishing each other a good night. The darkness was absolute and it seemed to heighten my senses to Holmes restless movements, however given my experiences in the war I found that such small noises were not enough to keep me from sleep. I was on the point of dropping off when Holmes voice roused me,

"I have one query, Watson, if I may."

"Yes?" I replied somewhat dozily.

"We have not known each other too long however I would offer that during the long hours of patient waiting during cases or in our rooms at Baker Street, I feel we have talked a great deal about a variety of subjects. Would you agree?"

"I would, Holmes. I've spent months with some chaps in the army where their past has remained more of a mystery to me through all of that time."

"My point exactly. But now I find that we are on a train to Edinburgh to stay with your cousin yet until a few days ago you had never mentioned him, and even then it was only to inform me of the briefest details of our proposed trip. I wonder why?" I lay in silence for a few seconds pondering the question,

"In truth Holmes, I had never given much thought to Patrick for some months and even less so before that. He had written after my return from Afghanistan to enquire of my health and asked what I was doing to occupy myself now that I was no longer in the service. That was before we had become acquainted and since then I have heard very little from him save his letter inviting me to Edinburgh, on which I accepted and informed him that you might also find the trip of benefit. He then sent me a telegram to confirm you were also very welcome. If I think about it logically, I think he was mostly concerned for my well being. Patrick is twenty years older than I, and he was injured quite seriously in the Crimean campaign. I was only a boy at the time but I do recall tales of his return from that war and that he had settled in Edinburgh. From his letters to me recently, I assume that when he heard I had been through a similar trauma with my injury that he wished to be a sympathetic ear and offer me some guidance in dealing with my new situation."

"A kindred spirit, Watson," Holmes replied thoughtfully, "sometimes a blessing but sometimes it can be a curse. Take care not to become one whose past is what defines them rather than the present and their future."

"I'm quite sure that won't be a problem, one thing about Patrick is that he is not a man who stands still. Since his return he has worked incredibly hard and has proven to be an accomplished and well respected surgeon. He is also employed as surgeon to the Queen when she visits Edinburgh so he is well known in the highest of circles." I paused to think back to my early memories of him, "From what little I recall of him he is a quiet man but very earnest. It's said now

that he is a greater surgeon even than Dr. Bell, more skilled with the scalpel at least if not in his powers of diagnostics."
"Have you met this Dr. Bell?" Holmes asked, I suspected trying to effect nonchalance.
"No," said I, "I've yet to have the privilege, but I hear he is quite an interesting fellow. He's certainly progressive in his teaching and I understand a firm believer in the new theories on antiseptic and cleanliness during surgery. Not to mention his advocacy for the nursing profession and giving his time to advancing their cause."
"Interesting, I shall look forward to meeting him." We fell silent again and even in the darkness I could sense in Holmes his longing to be back in our rooms at Baker Street where the possibility of a visitor would mean a case would have presented itself and the excitement of the chase would be upon him. This did not seem a good omen for our stay in Edinburgh but I consoled myself that once we arrived then he would be more in tune with himself again. I could not help thinking that he was somewhat preoccupied with the eminent Dr. Bell who would seem to be a match for Holmes intellect and method. However, such self doubt on Holmes part seemed so far removed from his character that I put it aside in my thoughts and drifted off to sleep with the steady rhythm of the train fading away to nothing.

Chapter 3

Our train pulled in at Waverley station on time at six o'clock on Monday morning, the date being the 22nd March 1882. I had slept quite well, being used to travelling over distance and the necessity to be rested and ready for action upon arrival. Holmes I guessed had slept only fitfully however this appeared to be usual for him as I would often hear him working in our front room at Baker Street in the early hours of the morning. Inevitably the scene which greeted me at breakfast time was akin to a bomb site, much to the disgust of Mrs. Hudson. I was about to ask Holmes how he had found the journey when a sharp whistle on the platform and a yell stopped me in my tracks. I raced to the window looking down the platform and saw a guard remonstrating with a passenger in a window further down. The train had barely come to a halt so I failed to see how there could be any argument already, especially since we were exactly on schedule. We disembarked and a porter came to assist us with our luggage,

"Patrick should be waiting for us, or if not be here very shortly," I said to Holmes. "His last telegram advised he would meet us from the train. Perhaps we should make our way out of the station to look for him." Holmes nodded and we instructed the porter to assist us with our bags who then dutifully led us off in the direction of the station exit. Passing by the guard who had shouted, and was still engaged in an argument with the same gentleman, my curiosity was piqued, "Tell me my good man," I addressed the porter, "do you know what that commotion is about? I couldn't help wonder since the guard seemed to shout at that passenger quite intently, in fact somewhat harshly I would suggest, so it's no

surprise they have come to blows." The porter glanced back at me,
"I'm not sure exactly sir, begging your pardon, but I heard someone tried to jump out of a carriage last night, before the train stopped, and he fell underneath and was dragged along by the wheels."
"Good God!" I replied.
"Aye sir, everyone's just a bit on edge now this mornin' and that passenger was in danger of meeting the same end. That's why he was on the receiving end from the guard." Holmes and I looked at each other but it was him that now spoke,
"This man who went under the train, do they believe it was an accident or an attempt at suicide?" he asked.
"Not sure sir, too early in the day and I've not had any chance to stop yet to find out more of the story from the tongue waggers." We walked on in silence until we exited the station and the porter deposited our bags on the pavement and left us to our own ends. I scanned around the cabs and carriages jostling for position outside but could not see any sign of a familiar face when a voice hollered to me from behind.
"John!" I turned to see a very smartly attired gentleman with a neat moustache and a military posture coming towards me. The family resemblance was uncanny and I knew at once this was my cousin. "John, splendid to meet you again," said Patrick as we shook hands warmly and then he turned to my companion, "and you must be Mr. Sherlock Holmes?" "I am, and it is a pleasure to make your acquaintance Dr. Watson." He in turn shook hands with Patrick who then pointed us in the direction of a waiting carriage. The coachman walked over and collected our bags as we climbed

aboard and made ourselves comfortable. Patrick was as I remembered him, polite, friendly but not overly effusive,
"I'm very glad you gentlemen could make it to Edinburgh. I trust you had a good journey?" We intimated that we had, although adding that a moving train is not the most conducive to a restful night's sleep, "I quite agree, I have on occasion taken the sleeper to London and back for medical matters and it does not sit well with me either. You shall have ample time to rest up during your stay here. Although I hope to be able to show you around the hospital and medical school while you are here John. Of course, you as well Mr Holmes, but I know that what we have here will be of particular interest to John being a doctor like myself." Holmes smiled graciously,
"Quite so, I should be most interested also but I am here in the main to keep my eye on Watson that he does not get up to any mischief." I laughed at this remark, knowing as Holmes did that the opposite was true, but I did not elaborate to my cousin,
"I'm very much looking forward to it Patrick," said I, "and meeting your family as well." We continued to exchange pleasantries as we rode along our route and at the same time Patrick was acting as tour guide, pointing out the landmarks and asking his driver to take us by some of the more famous of these as we went.
The carriage trundled along Princes Street with its wonderful open gardens along one side and past the magnificent Scott Monument towering above the street. Our eyes were drawn magnetically past this to the castle beyond, which could not have been more fortuitously placed if it had been planned by Robert Adam himself. Its aspect from the top of the volcanic rock was stunning and its shadow was cast over the old town

close by, over the park down below and I would expect even over the rooftops of the exquisite New Town. I sneaked a quick sideways glance at Holmes who was leaning forward on his seat to see more clearly out of the window. I was momentarily impressed that the sights of Edinburgh could command the attention of Sherlock Holmes, when I realised that he was not in fact admiring the castle but his gaze was darting all over, locking the details of the place, the people, the city itself away in his mind for later use if required.

Our journey took us along Princes Street, turning up around by the Castle and down what I learned to be the High Street and finally back in the direction of Princes Street. Much to Holmes' chagrin, and Patrick's amusement, I would every now and then ask the driver to stop to allow me to step outside for a moment to more fully take in the sights. Despite Holmes' interest in our surroundings he would make an exasperated sigh at each of these occasions and slump dramatically back into his seat until we were again on the move. Our tour continued to Leith and the less than salubrious sights of the docks with a grimy cloud hanging over the bulkers as they discharged their cargoes, attended to by the rough types of men which I found were best avoided and which Holmes found of infinite interest. Ironically, as I was at the point where I would have been happy to ask our host to return us to the centre of the city, Holmes interest was awakened and he again sat forward to drink in every detail. Having satisfied ourselves with this we were taken back towards the city and onward in the direction of my cousin's house.

I settled back into my seat, content that I had seen enough for the moment, as Patrick did likewise. “What do you make of our old city then Mr Holmes?” asked Patrick, “Quite an impressive sight is it not?” Holmes nodded,
“It is indeed impressive, Doctor Watson. I must confess that I have seen a great number of interesting sights since we arrived and have sought to commit them all to my memory in order to have a better understanding of the city.” I smiled broadly at this,
“You see Holmes, I knew you would enjoy being in Edinburgh once you had a chance to see it. What did you make of the Scott Monument? I don’t think I have ever seen an example of such intricate and well crafted masonry in a long time.” Holmes gave me a slightly vague look,
“In all honesty, Watson, the building itself did not interest me, although I did glance at it momentarily. It was a fine sight indeed.” He glanced nonchalantly back towards the window,
“Goodness Holmes, it didn’t interest you? Here was I thinking you were taking in all of the sights Edinburgh has to offer and you were doing no such thing.” He turned to me again, this time with a piercing glance,
“Watson, it seems that you are blinkered to all but the obvious again. With respect to you Doctor Watson,” he now addressed my cousin, “please forgive my harsh tone in this instance.” Patrick nodded politely, “Thank-you,” continued Holmes, “as I was saying, with all respect this is a fine city but my interests can sometimes lie parallel to those of others.” He smiled curtly at me, “Tell me, Watson, while we were passing the monument, did you happen to notice the beggar sitting at the foot of the West side of the building, the

one who had fallen on hard times since leaving the Navy? Or perhaps the two doctors who were taking an early morning stroll through the gardens? Or even the young lad who picked the pocket of one of those Doctors, making off with his money clip?" I shook my head and looked towards Patrick who laughed,
"I think he has you there, John? I must confess I saw none of those either."
"I think he does. Holmes you are a wonder. You would not bat an eyelid at a platoon of soldiers marching past, yet you would be able to tell me what size boots they were wearing." I laughed also now, "Most definitely a wonder!" Holmes smiled mischievously,
"I shall take that as a compliment, Watson." He laughed briefly and turned back towards the window. I was about to add a further remark when Holmes suddenly lashed out with his cane, striking the top of the carriage three times, "Halloa! Driver, stop here!" he yelled as he leaned out of the window looking back along the direction from which we had just come. A moment later he had unlatched the door and was stepping out of the carriage with Patrick and I quickly following at his heels.
"What on earth is going on Holmes?" I demanded. He silenced me with a finger placed swiftly across his lips and then used it to point further down the street. My eyes followed the line of his hand to a house where a small crowd of onlookers were gathered on the pavement outside.
The heavy black front door of the Georgian townhouse stood wide open and outside there was a police constable and what looked to be an older policeman in plain clothes next to him, judging by the pen and notebook in his hand. Although we

could not hear their conversation from this distance it was clear that the younger man was being given a dressing down by his superior. Standing in the road was a hearse of the most basic kind and as we stood watching, two men whom I presumed were the undertaker and his assistant went into the house. Patrick leaned in and whispered to us,
"That, gentlemen, is possibly the most talked about house in Edinburgh at the moment, and I would expect that by the look of the events before us, that is a situation that will only increase."
"Why? What's the story with the house?" I asked.
"Well, the story goes that the house is haunted." I turned to look at Patrick to ensure that he was being serious but it appeared that he was. Holmes continued to look at the house,
"In what way is it haunted?" he asked.
"I'm not entirely sure of the facts Mr Holmes, but I believe the Police have been there for some weeks and have yet to get to the bottom of the matter. I've not the time to take too much notice in this type of thing but now that we seem to have a death on our hands then it makes it more likely. Either Doctor Bell or myself will most likely carry out the post mortem examination if there are suspicious circumstances involved."
"I should say it looks suspicious," said I, "What do you make of it Holmes?" He said nothing but motioned for us to keep watching. The older policeman had disappeared inside the house and the younger man was pacing around at the foot of the front steps, wringing his hands furiously. When the older man returned to the steps and gestured to his subordinate to move the onlookers away, he seemed to glance in our direction and then stop. I was sure that I saw his posture

stiffen and he turned and said something to the constable who then also looked in our direction.
“I believe the older man is a detective officer, Watson. Something here is definitely amiss.” At that moment, a coffin was carried out and unceremoniously loaded into the back of the hearse with the two men then climbing up to their positions ready to move off. The detective walked around and spoke to them before the hearse set off in the opposite direction from our position with the detective also clambering onboard. At this same moment, a lady wearing a green dress appeared in the doorway and was clearly in a state of distress, weeping into her handkerchief. A maid stood next to her trying to offer her consolation as they both watched the hearse move off and remove the departed from the scene.
“I assume that is the widow,” said I, “perhaps we should move on Holmes and not intrude upon her grief.” Holmes nodded and we returned to our carriage where I opened the door for Patrick to enter and then Holmes, but before Holmes embarked he stopped and looked around. My eyes again followed the line of his and I saw the weeping woman and the maid returning into the house, and the onlookers began to disperse slowly as they exchanged views on what they had witnessed. His superior having departed, the young police constable had remained standing outside and was still looking in our direction. Holmes tipped his hat towards the man and then climbed into the carriage as I followed, closing the door behind me. The carriage jolted into movement as Patrick instructed the driver to take us to his home.

Chapter 4

The house in Charlotte Square where we now found ourselves was a magnificent Georgian building, its classical Greek architecture on the façade giving it an appropriate grandeur.

"Athens of the North indeed, Watson," my friend remarked as we stood admiring the building. Patrick smiled graciously,

"I'm very fortunate gentlemen to be able to live in somewhat comfortable surroundings. But please come in and let me introduce you to my wife and family, the real reason I count myself a fortunate man." As we walked up the steps a smartly dressed young footman greeted us and Patrick directed him to take our luggage to our rooms. The entrance hallway was every bit as grand as the front of the building suggested it would be, but one thing that I immediately noticed was the furniture consisted of modest pieces and the décor was warm but not overly fussy as is sometimes the style in such houses. I believed this was as much a sign of the straightforward character of my cousin as it was the good taste of his wife, both of which were to be much admired.

At that point we heard a woman's footsteps on the stairs and Patrick greeted her affectionately. "Elizabeth my dear, let me introduce you to my cousin, Doctor John Watson." She smiled at me in a most disarming way that made me feel immediately welcome in their home,

"John, I am delighted to meet you after all this time." I reciprocated with a friendly smile,

"The pleasure is mine Elizabeth. May I also introduce my friend, Mr Sherlock Holmes." Her eyes shifted to Holmes whom she regarded curiously, almost as if trying to reconcile

the image which she had in her mind with that of the reality standing before her.
“Mr. Holmes, it is a pleasure to meet you.” Holmes nodded and replied in kind, “I hope that you had a pleasant journey?”
“Thank-you, yes, the train was fine, in fact we have had a more eventful journey from the station to your home if I am honest.” Elizabeth looked towards Patrick, confused at my friend’s remark,
“We had the occasion to pass the Turner house at a very inopportune moment. Or in Mr. Holmes’ case I believe it may have been a very opportune moment?” Patrick offered.
“Indeed, it was certainly of interest,” Holmes replied, “but as my friend here is apt to remind me, we are here on holiday and I should not involve myself in any local matters. But I would be intrigued to hear a little more of the story behind this if you will indulge me?” Patrick was about to answer when Elizabeth beat him to the punch,
“Mr. Holmes, nothing would give me greater pleasure, although perhaps we should let you and John settle in? You’ve had a tiring journey and I’m sure you would like to take some rest?”
“That would be very agreeable,” said I, “I think I should perhaps like to take a quick nap to recoup my energies.” Elizabeth looked towards Holmes who did not seem taken with the idea of rest but in any event agreed that it would indeed be a good idea. We gave our thanks to Patrick who was shortly to depart for the hospital to start his work for the day, and Elizabeth led us up the staircase towards our rooms.
“You must be very proud of Patrick,” said I, “I’ve read some great things in the medical journals about his work here. I’m looking forward to getting to know him a little better in

person." She didn't turn around but I could tell she was smiling as she replied,
"Yes, he has done very well here. I know he is also keen to become better acquainted, especially since you have such a lot in common such as your medicine and your experiences in the war. I hope that you are recovering quite well?" I replied that I was and told her of my current situation with Holmes in Baker Street and she was most intrigued,
"You seem to have quite an eventful life now, and you also Mr. Holmes?"
"Yes, thank-you, quite eventful," he replied, "it has been a most fortunate coming together with Watson and myself. He is certainly an agreeable companion and seems able to put up with my, what shall we say Watson? Peculiarities?" I laughed heartily,
"Hah, yes I think we could definitely say that."
Elizabeth showed us to our respective rooms and bade us a pleasant rest before returning downstairs. I closed my bedroom door and a moment afterwards I heard Holmes' door also close. I eased myself onto the bed and allowed the comfortable mattress and bedding to embrace me, and shortly afterwards drifted off into a deep and satisfying sleep. For Holmes' part I am unsure exactly what he was about during the afternoon but I did not hear him leave his room so I can only assume he did likewise.

I woke later in the afternoon feeling much more rested and made my way downstairs, having not received any reply to my knocking on Holmes' door. As I turned at the bottom of the staircase towards the parlour I could hear male voices drifting out through the door which was slightly ajar, one of whom I instantly recognised as Holmes. I went into the room and was faced with Sherlock Holmes standing in front of the fire, smoking on his pipe as if he were in his own front room, and in the chair opposite my cousin sat similarly drawing deeply on his pipe. "I see the party is in full swing?" I said cheerily.

"Indeed Watson," Holmes replied, "I regret we could not wait any longer for you to come out of your hibernation. Your cousin has been most gracious in listening to some of my tales and we have been discussing various medical matters of which your opinion will be most heartily sought over dinner." Patrick gestured me to a chair and prepared drinks for the three of us,

"John, you look a little better after your rest. I must admit that I was a little concerned for your health when I saw you this morning. However, looking at you now I would put that down to your rather tiring overnight journey. Do you feel well enough?"

"Oh as well as I can expect," I replied, "I have a few aches now and again but on the whole I feel I am on the mend. My fitness continues to improve," I said, pointing to Holmes, "as this gentleman sees that I keep on my feet and have no opportunity for squandering my time." Holmes smiled and gestured his pipe from his eyes and then in my direction to signify he was indeed keeping me under observation. Patrick laughed,

"It is good to see you back and settled into normal life again. I can't tell you the number of times I've seen men come back from the war and they are lost to drink or opium and are but a shell of the men they once were. I had to operate only this morning on a man who had fallen under a train at the station, apparently an accident but one can never tell. It may have been an attempt to end his life since he had also recently returned from battle. But I fear that his scars were of a more mental nature and far deeper than you or I have had to endure John." Holmes and I looked at each other briefly in a moment of recognition,

"Aah, so you were operating on that man?" I asked, "we noticed some evidence of the aftermath of the accident when we arrived this morning. Tell me, did he live?" Patrick's face darkened slightly,

"He did, although the train had crushed his bones beyond any repair so I had no option but to amputate both of his legs. I fear he will have a worse time of it now than he has already endured, however his life is saved which is a sign that God has not yet allowed him to serve out his full purpose." We contemplated this news for a moment and although none of our party knew the man we could feel some empathy for his situation. It was Holmes who broke our contemplation,

"As we are speaking of incidents, Doctor Watson, your good wife told me she would fill me in on the details of the activity we witnessed in," he paused, "what was the name of the road again Watson?"

"Heriot Row." I replied, knowing only too well that this was not asked to remind Holmes, but his insufferable way of ensuring my observational faculties had been deployed.

"That's it, thank-you, yes, in Heriot Row. However I must confess my curiosity is beginning to increase and I wonder if you would oblige me?"

"Well, there was some talk of it at the hospital today but very few details were known. In fact it has only added to the mystery surrounding what I mentioned is already the most talked about household in Edinburgh at the moment. At least when I say most talked about, that is only in the police and scientific circles and a few select others who are aware of the matter." Holmes took a few steps to another chair and, flaring out his coat tails with a waft of his hands, he sat down and looked intently at my cousin,

"How so?" he asked, trying to effect an air of innocent curiosity, of which I was more than accustomed and knew that Sherlock Holmes' interest had most definitely been piqued.

"Well, Mr Holmes," Patrick continued, "for the past few months there have been reports of, how can I put it, strange goings on in that house. What I mean to say is that the house would seem to have become haunted." I let out a scornful snort,

"Haunted? There's no such thing." said I. Holmes had maintained his focus and waited for the next piece of the story, as Patrick explained further,

"Exactly my thoughts too, John, but so far the police have carried out weeks of investigation but would seem to be no further forward. As far as I am aware the whole business started when the lady of the house, Mrs Victoria Turner, heard some knocking noises in the night. I believe at first her husband was able to persuade her that the noises were only those of the servants or perhaps the house settling into the cool night. I think since he had not heard anything himself he just assumed she had been subject to a nightmare, but the following night when Mrs Turner awoke and heard the knocking again she shook Mr. Turner and he too heard the noise. From there I do not know much more I'm afraid but all

I can tell you is that this went on for some weeks and then the Turners were able to call in the police to investigate, yet they have not come up with any solution to the problem." Holmes was still in his same position, his grey eyes focused on Patrick but his mind elsewhere as he digested what limited information he had been given. I myself walked around and sat on a chair to ease the ache in my leg,
"I take it they did not find that any of the servants were involved in causing the noise?" I asked.
"No, nothing, and none of the servants have been able to shed any light on the incidents either. In all honesty I have heard that they are now considering that this may be a genuine case of supernatural occurrence and outside of their remit to resolve the matter." Holmes sat back and looked thoughtfully at the fire,
"So we can only assume then gentlemen, if that is the case then this Edinburgh ghost has claimed a victim during the night" said he, "I take it you did not hear of the identity of the corpse?"
"No. The police are keeping a very tight rein on any information on the case. I understand the detective in charge was under great pressure not to waste too many valuable resources on what they saw as a wild goose chase so he had in turn passed responsibility to a young constable but word has it he does not have the experience to resolve the matter. I have very little time to become too involved in the gossip surrounding it you understand, but from what little I have heard there may be something in this which is beyond our ken Mr Holmes. 'There is more on heaven and earth' as they say. What do you think Mr. Holmes?" My friend now looked blasé at the prospect of giving this matter any great attention,

"In all honesty I feel there must be a very simple explanation to all of this. I would lay the blame for the prolonged nature of the investigation at the door of the Edinburgh Police, and in trusting the case to someone clearly out of his depth. What is the name of this young constable?"
"Morthouse," replied Patrick, "James Morthouse." Holmes laughed dryly,
"This Morthouse must surely be missing some key piece of evidence which has presented itself and he has not had the attention to notice."
"Do you think it's that simple Holmes?" said I, "The officers here I am sure are every bit as good as those we have in London." He stood up suddenly and returned to the fire,
"My point exactly, Watson! However I am heartened to find that Edinburgh has more than its fair share of intrigue."
"How so?" I asked, "Has there been something more?" Holmes rifled around a small pile of newspapers left by the fire and handed one to me,
"A suspicious death Watson, albeit most likely caused by an explosion due to leaking gas in the home but evidence again of some event that is, shall we say, more of my kind of interest?"
"The article you have here Holmes does suggest the police have closed the matter, surely you don't plan to become involved in this?"
"Hah, no Watson, I am merely heartened that there lies beneath the genteel streets of Edinburgh the same beating heart which we have in London." I rolled my eyes towards Patrick and threw the paper back down to the floor,
"Holmes, honestly!" said I.

Our conversation about the case and other matters of the criminal kind tailed off in due course and the subjects turned to more mundane matters when we were joined by Elizabeth and the children for a time. Presently we organised ourselves and left the house for dinner as Patrick and Elizabeth treated Holmes and I to a lovely meal in one of their favourite restaurants in town. I found my cousin to be pleasant company and it was refreshing for me to discuss medical matters again with a fellow physician. I had Holmes as company in London of course, with whom I could discuss such matters, however as much as he would sneer at me for saying it, his amateur knowledge was not comparable, in my view, to those of us who have studied the subject professionally. I was aware that Patrick was spoiled for choice with medical colleagues with whom to discuss the issues of the day, mostly more eminent than I, but I believe we both enjoyed the opportunity to get to know one another through our mutual interest. I found Patrick to be a fascinating man, highly principled and judging by his accounts of the operations he had performed he was an accomplished surgeon. In between the talk of the university and that world, Elizabeth would press Holmes to recount some stories of his investigations in London and would relish the atmosphere he created in depicting the darker side of our fellow man and their deeds. The tales of dank nights filled with an unholy fog, tracking his quarry and cornering them like a sewer rat until it was a matter of handing them over to the police, filled her with horror and excitement in equal measure.

Once we had adjourned from dinner we took a cab to the Morningside Athenaeum for a piano recital given by a talented young lady named Helen Hopekirk who was accompanied by an astounding vocalist. The programme moved from Bach to Beethoven with some pieces by Chopin woven into their repertoire. I was enthralled by the playing and I could see that Holmes also was lost in his enjoyment of the performance, as his eyes were closed and his expression one of earnest focus. I knew that with Holmes' dedication to his craft, he appreciated anyone who could show similar aptitude in their chosen field and Miss Hopekirk's technique on the piano was a glimpse at perfection, not to mention her intuitive perception of the composers' intent in the music.

Once the concert had ended, Holmes wished to go and pass on his praise to the pianist and Elizabeth went to the stage with him also to make her appreciation known to both performers. Patrick and I remained in our seats for the time being and watched them pick their way through the small gathering to make their way to the front. "You're a very lucky man, Patrick." I said as we watched them go, "Elizabeth is a fine woman and you have struck up quite a comfortable life here." He nodded thoughtfully,

"Very true John, and I would not change my situation for all the tea in China. With a wife and children, I feel it makes a man complete and my work seems to fulfil every other need I have within me." He turned and looked at me curiously, "I am surprised that you are not back in the profession yet, John. You have been back for long enough now that you could surely have found a practice with which to work or even find a residence in a hospital?"

"Well," said I, "in truth I may find my way back to medicine yet, but at the moment I am content enough. My injuries have healed well, albeit I am not as limber as I was, but for some reason I do not feel ready quite yet to return to practice. I'm sure you must understand that?" He looked towards the stage again, avoiding my gaze,

"To a certain extent, I can. But what I also understand, John, is that a man must have something with which to devote his life towards and at the moment I do not see that within you. I would not wish to see you go downhill as did my patient this morning whose world was collapsing around him. You are a skilled physician and I would hate to see that go to waste." He smiled warmly and put his hand on my arm, "Please understand that my only concern is for your well being. I know more than anyone the situation you are in since my path has been a prelude to the one that you are now on." I could sense that he was genuinely concerned for my welfare at which I was touched. It had been so long since I had been in contact with any family that it was a blessing to find that such a caring individual was in my corner.

"Patrick, I am grateful for your concern but for the moment I have my work with Holmes to occupy me and my medical training comes in very useful at times I can assure you. I am certain at some point I shall return to practice but for the moment I am quite content documenting Holmes cases and assisting him where I can."

"Very well, I hope you did not mind me asking?" I shook my head and waved dismissively as he continued, "but I am glad to hear that you have plans to return to medicine. One never knows when an opportunity to do so can arise and it is of comfort to me you would not immediately pass it up without consideration." I was about to question Patrick on this statement when Holmes and Elizabeth returned and my focus shifted to them.

“My dear Doctors Watson,” Holmes said to us, more cheerily that he had sounded since we had arrived, “it has been a delightful evening and now Elizabeth informs me she is exhausted and would like us all to retire back to your lovely home. I must say I am inclined to agree since my friend here,” said he, gesturing in my direction, “also looks ready to drop and has a most concerning pallor. So I feel we should make our way back and rest ourselves for the night, ready to greet the new day and all that it may bring.”

Chapter 5

I awoke early the next morning after a night's sleep which had been punctuated by short periods of insomnia as I mulled over in my mind my conversation with Patrick the evening before, and on my reasons for not returning sooner to medicine. It was frustrating that despite these nocturnal episodes I could not come to a satisfactory answer to my question. In normal circumstances I could have mildly pointed out to my questioner that they had no concept of the scars which one brings back from a war like that but in the case of my cousin it was not a road which would lead to any fruitful conclusion. Patrick had recovered from his injuries which had been sustained in the Crimea and in due course had taken up his career again and had become one of the most respected surgeons in Edinburgh which was no mean feat. Testament of which was in the high regard he was held by Dr. Bell and the other luminaries of the medical school. I consoled myself again with the knowledge that within myself I did not yet feel the enthusiasm to return to medicine and in fact my current occupation was providing me with as much, if not more, stimulation than I required. Although in the back of mind there was now a nagging voice which had been set in motion by Patrick that made me wonder if this was indeed the best path for me to tread.

We met in the dining room for breakfast at seven thirty with Holmes, Patrick, Elizabeth and I still discussing the performance from the night before. Elizabeth had hoped we would be able to catch another performance in the city before we left and Holmes and I shared this wish most assuredly. The breakfast was a traditional and hearty one consisting of salmon, eggs and a strong tea which was surely intended to put us on a firm footing for the day and offer us protection from the Scottish weather outside. Although the day was fine and clear there was a definite chill wind blowing through the city which I was not accustomed to in London. I found it curious that within such a small country as ours the differences could be so great but at the same time the similarities bound us inextricably together. Patrick completed his meal and placed his napkin on the table, "John, I wondered if you would like to accompany me to the medical school and hospital today for a tour? I'm sure you would find it most interesting."

"I would be delighted," I replied, somewhat more enthusiastically than I intended which took me a little by surprise, "I've heard many stories of the school and it would be a fascinating place to see. Would you care to join us Holmes?" Holmes took a sip of his tea for a moment before replying,

"Well, Watson, that is a most gracious invitation however I would not wish to intrude into such an outing. Although, it may prove interesting so I must confess I am tempted." Both Patrick and I assured him that it would be no intrusion and that he was most welcome. He continued, "I wonder if we might meet Dr. Bell while we are there?"

"I'm unsure of Dr. Bell's schedule for today, I must admit, so I do not know his movements." said Patrick, "But I am pleased to tell you that we have been invited to dine with him this evening. All of us, that is." I looked towards Holmes who was looking intriguingly pleased,

"Excellent! Then if that is the case I shall decline your invitation for today's outing and save myself for this evening.

I'm sure it will be a most engaging dinner party." At this, Elizabeth stood to leave the table and informed us that she would unfortunately be unable to attend due to family matters but wished us to pass her regards to Dr. Bell. Patrick and I stood to leave also but Holmes remained seated at the table, drinking his tea,
"What will you do with yourself today Holmes?" I asked, "Surely you would be better to come with Patrick and I rather than squander a day sitting here?" Patrick joined me in echoing this sentiment,
"It would be an honour to show you the facilities we have here Mr Holmes. I must apologise that sometimes my work draws me in too close and I forget that it is not always of interest to all of my guests." Holmes smiled and waved his hand dismissively,
"Not at all, Doctor Watson, I am well aware of how these things can keep one fully occupied. I am in a similar situation with my own profession. I fancy that the demands of the two are not too far removed from one another, wouldn't you say?" Patrick nodded politely, and I felt somewhat diplomatically, and excused himself to speak to his wife while I took the opportunity to sit back down and drink the remainder of my tea with Holmes. I used to be a sociable fellow but, despite my increasing interest to see the medical school, there was still a part of me that would gladly exchange the opportunity and our comfortable rooms here to be back in our lodgings at Baker Street, poised over the daily newspapers pondering the issues of the day. I looked over at Holmes who was watching me carefully,
"What is it Holmes?" said I. He smiled,

“Your cousin seems very intent to bring you into his world of medicine Watson, perhaps he has some ulterior motive? You may end up with a stethoscope around your neck before the day is out.”
“Don’t talk rubbish Holmes,” I retorted, “it makes perfect sense given my background that I would be interested to take in the medical establishments. It would be much the same if you were offered the chance to view the workings of a world renowned police department, would it not?” He let out a short laugh,
“Hah, I have yet to encounter one of those Watson, but yes, I take your point.”
“What are your plans for the day then Holmes?” He stood and strode over to the window, looking first left and then right up the street outside,
“If my observations are correct Watson, I believe we may be about to discover just that. If you will excuse me my friend, I believe I may have a visitor approaching.” At that moment a clear high pitched bell rang out to indicate someone at the front door,
”Holmes, we are not at Baker Street now, the visitor will surely be here to see Patrick or Elizabeth? I am sure that no-one in Edinburgh even knows we are here.” He pressed a finger to his lips and waved a hand to quieten me, and in doing so we could hear voices in the hallway outside. Firstly one of the servants and then Patrick could be heard, along with a person unknown to me who was quietly spoken, but a detectable tremble was growing in her voice as the discussion continued. I was about to protest that we should not be eavesdropping on our host when the door to the breakfast room opened and Patrick entered,

"Mr. Holmes," he said, "it seems you have visitors."

I closed the door on Holmes and his visitors and gave Patrick a shrug to indicate that I was as much in the dark as he was about the circumstances by which this had come about. Patrick had shown them into his study, an oak panelled room with a consulting desk across one corner, in front of which were two chairs which the visitors had been occupying as I left. 'Would you like me to stay, Holmes?' I had enquired, I must admit somewhat hopefully, but Holmes had waved me away insisting that it was not necessary and he would not wish me to miss my outing today on his account. While I appreciated the sentiment I could not help feeling a little aggrieved that here was a matter which, if it had arisen in London, we would have tackled together with my taking down the particulars, but here it seemed that Holmes had dispensed with my services. Patrick and I left the house moments later and were soon in a hansom trotting through Edinburgh on our way to the medical school as our first port of call. I sat quietly as we rode, looking out of the window as we passed back along Princes Street, the people of Edinburgh already about their business and although busy in the streets there did not seem to be the same frantic bustle as we encountered in London. My thoughts were back in the study in Patrick's house wondering what exactly was taking place and I knew that I was missing being in my usual Boswell role to Holmes.

"You seem very quiet this morning John." Patrick asked, jolting me from my reflections, "I trust that you slept well and nothing was amiss with your breakfast?" I was momentarily flustered to think that I was being most

ungracious towards my cousin, with whom I was keen to become better acquainted, and here I sat becoming introspective over some issue which was none of my business.
"Goodness, no Patrick, no everything has been most agreeable. I can't thank you enough for your and Elizabeth's hospitality. I hope you don't mind that I invited Holmes to accompany me?"
"Not at all, he seems like an interesting man albeit a little difficult to read at times. I find his choice of career to be a curious one, especially with the police's use of him in their difficult moments." I looked puzzled,
"How so?" I asked
"Well, John, to be frank, I suppose that I, and in fact we, are from a profession that does not take kindly to amateurs, no matter how gifted in their study, from becoming involved in medical matters. If I were encountering some difficulty in my performance of a procedure I would not call in one who was unqualified in our field to advise me upon it. But with Mr. Holmes and the police the complete opposite seems to be the case. I can only assume that he is either a truly gifted amateur or the police in London are not of great resource." I could see the point that Patrick was making and in truth the parallel when applied to medicine did seem preposterous but I did not believe that it was entirely fair,
"Your point is well made," said I, "but the difference here is that Holmes is no mere amateur in his field. He has a gifted mind and has studied areas of investigation that the police have not yet even alighted upon as being of use in their profession. I would more compare Holmes with the early pioneers of medicine who pushed back the boundaries and in

doing so were at great odds with established thinking of the time. That is the only way I can explain Holmes' superiority over the police." Patrick smiled and nodded,
"He is lucky to have someone to come so staunchly to his defence. You seem to have formed a good friendship there which is to be commended. I must confess I am looking forward to Mr. Holmes meeting with Dr. Bell this evening, it should prove to be most enlightening for us watching as involved bystanders so to speak."
"You seem to know something I do not Patrick as I assume that we will also be involved in the discussions tonight? After all, I do not anticipate that we should sit quietly in the shadows."
"Oh, quite right John," he said smiling, "but I believe our part may be more as referees in the game than as active participants in the moves." I let the matter go, unable to fathom this rather cryptic reply which I would more have expected from Holmes than my cousin.
A short time later we turned right from the main road on which we were travelling and went through a large stone archway and I was met with the sight of magnificent buildings all around me fronted with Grecian style arches and pillars and being within an enclosed courtyard the effect was quite stunning.
"This is the Edinburgh University, John, and within these walls is one of the greatest schools of medicine in the world."
Our cab came to a stop in the centre of the quadrangle and we alighted with Patrick leading me across the courtyard into one of the buildings. Inside I was led along corridors which seemed to speak to me with their history, the busts of previous alumni and pioneers watching me carefully as I

strolled past them, their combined achievements standing testimony to the reputation of this place. We walked past several lecture halls before Patrick opened the door of a further hall and looked inside, before turning to me and smiling,
"We are in luck, Dr. Bell is just completing one of his addresses. Come in and we can wait at the side until he finishes." I followed Patrick through the door, closing it gently behind me, and we shuffled along the wall as the class was in progress. I scanned along the rows of eager faces, listening intently to the lecture, and my eyes then fell around upon the object of their attention. Dr. Joseph Bell was a thin man with curly white hair and an almost gaunt face with sharp features. He was joined at the front by a jocular looking man, shabbily dressed and his head bandaged heavily. He had a look of stunned shock on his face as Dr. Bell seemed to continue to tell him fact after fact about his person, his recent engagements and travel and on some members of his close family. 'But how do you know all of this!' he cried, at which Dr. Bell merely remarked, as much to his students as to the man, 'one must never forget the great significance of the trifling details, my good man. Such as this button on your coat, clearly this has been made from ivory and is hand carved thereby I have deduced that you were in Africa recently, since the colouration of the button is of new appearance,' and then turning to address his students, 'look well upon this man all of you, since for your next appearance in my lecture hall I wish you to tell me, from what you see before you now, this mans profession and why he was recently in Lanark.' The man again looked shocked but was drowned out by the stampede of feet on the wooden floor as

the students cascaded out into the corridor outside. Patrick and I walked over and I was introduced, to which Dr. Bell reciprocated,
"Very nice to meet you Doctor Watson," he laughed easily, "I hope you did not think my little demonstration arrogant, but I feel that in order to instil in my students the discipline to examine the details closely, it impresses them if I lead by example." I shook my head,
"Not at all, in fact I have seen a similar demonstration from a friend of mine."
"Aah yes," said he, "I understand I shall have the privilege to meet Mr. Sherlock Holmes this evening? I must admit that the newspapers in Edinburgh do not carry much news of his work in London but I hear through your discussions with Patrick that he is much sought after?"
"Indeed, although much to my annoyance, but to Holmes amusement, his name is nearly always kept out of the news and his involvement is rarely known by the general public. I would find this to be most aggravating but, as I say, Holmes seems unperturbed by it." Dr. Bell nodded thoughtfully,
"Clearly a man for whom the work is in itself reward enough. I shall look forward to meeting him. Now, I am afraid you must excuse me gentlemen. I have been called in to perform a post mortem on a victim for the police and I believe there is some suspicious circumstance."
"Which victim is that?" Patrick enquired, "John and Mr. Holmes were witness to a body being removed from a house in Heriot Row on their way from the station yesterday. I was with them but I could not tell them anything of the circumstances surrounding it, other than those that are widely known. I suspect that you may be a man with more in the

way of information on the matter." Joseph Bell's face took on a mischievous quality which I have also recognised in Holmes, that look that suggests that nothing would be easier than to answer the question, but it would be much more interesting to meddle with those asking the said question,
"Well, gentlemen, I think in that case we may have our first topic of discussion for this evening but for now I must keep my own counsel until I have performed my duty. I do not wish to start to throw out theories and ideas in case they cloud my reading of the actual facts as I find them. I'm sure you understand." With that he collected his hat and coat and bade us farewell until we would meet again at seven o'clock at his home in Melville Street that night.
Patrick waited until the door had closed behind Dr. Bell and then took to one of the seats normally occupied by the students,
"So what is your first impression of Dr. Bell, John?" I leaned against the heavy desk on the dais in the front of the room,
"He seems a pleasant enough fellow," I replied genuinely, "but I believe I now have a better understanding of your earlier remark – it would seem that we will have an interesting evening." He smiled,
"I heartily agree. But what of our facility here, John, do you like what you see? As you know we have access not only to some of the greatest minds in medicine but our facilities here are as much a boon to our success as is the quality of our faculty." I glanced around the room, admiring the wealth of information adorning the walls and the laboratory equipment similarly displayed,

"Again, I am very impressed. It was certainly worth the trip to Edinburgh to see this and I have only scratched the surface." He stood up and walked over towards me,
"Absolutely John, there is so much more to see. However, I will tell you of one problem we have at the moment. Our students are lacking in the tutorship in the field of battle injuries, of field medicine, of medicine as it must be performed on the front lines. While many of them will no doubt end up in a comfortable practice somewhere, we feel that it would benefit them all to learn such matters as it gives them a whole new perspective on what is possible under the most trying of circumstances. You know only too well John that the genteel world of medical practice is often overtaken by the urgency and improvisation required by the situation on the field."
"I can well attest to that." I remarked, "But they must be glad of your experience in the field Patrick, are they not?" He shook his head, frowning,
"Unfortunately my time is now taken up with other matters and between my surgery work and the matters pertaining to the running of the medical school I do not have time to take this in hand. There is no-one else currently within our staff that has the necessary experience first hand. You can see our problem?" I raised my eyebrows and pondered this,
"I do indeed. I recall when I was in Afghanistan there was a field surgeon by the name of Ashington who I believe has returned to this country. I am unsure of his exact whereabouts but I did run into his batman some weeks back and he mentioned he had moved to the Yorkshire area. I could perhaps…" I stopped as Patrick held up his hand,

"John, I don't believe you have taken my meaning. We do not wish to seek out someone for the post, for I would like you to take this post." I was stunned,
"Me? But how would that be possible, especially since I live in London?"
"Provision can be made for your relocation to Edinburgh, John. Nothing would be easier and I can think of no-one better suited to the post than you." I said nothing as thoughts raced through my mind. Here was I, only two days into my meeting with Patrick and I am being offered a position five hundred miles from home. This would certainly secure my return to a medical position, but what of Holmes, what of my work with him? I thought back to his casual dismissal of my company earlier in the morning. I am sure he would not be lost for long without my assistance I supposed. I glanced at Patrick again,
"So this is the reason for my invitation to Edinburgh? The offer of a position here?" He shook his head and held out his hands,
"Of course not John, my invitation was made to you with the best of intentions and I am sincerely glad that we have been able to become better acquainted. But perhaps this is a case of luck being the residue of design, as the discussions of the post only arose in any seriousness after I had extended my invitation to you. I am sorry if it seems there was any subterfuge, but on my recommendation the board of governors have approved me to make you this offer. What do you say, John? Lecturer in Battlefield Medicine Techniques and a fine salary to accompany the title? Will you at least consider the post?" I was about to dismiss it out of hand, but something within prevented me from doing so.

"Let me view more of what Edinburgh has to offer Patrick, and then you shall have my answer…"

PART 2

A Recent History of Constable James Morthouse

Chapter 6

As Sherlock Holmes and John Watson were arriving at Waverley station on that Monday morning, Constable James Morthouse was standing on the front steps of the Turner house in Heriot Row wondering quite why this was happening to him and, in no small measure, wondering exactly how the next few moments would unfold. The frantic activity inside the house was understandable but he could not escape the feeling that the finger of blame for this incident would be pointed squarely at him. He was acutely aware that his first few weeks in the Edinburgh City Police had not been blessed with great success and in fact, if it were open to subjective argument, the very opposite could be said to be true. It had been only two days ago that he had felt the full force of his sergeant's anger after an incident involving a theft, which had left his colleague injured. Thinking back he could still feel his inner ear flinch with the force of the sound which had assaulted him. This was not to infer that Morthouse had been at fault, however this would not deter his superior from taking the opportunity to issue him with a stern reprimand.

Morthouse glanced across the steps to where another constable had joined him to ensure no curious onlookers tried to sidle in too close to the house. Williams was someone whom Morthouse had been paired with when signing on to the police in order to allow the man's greater experience to transfer to him, but the pairing had been short lived after

Morthouse was put on to the special assignment which now brought him to stand outside the Turner house. This was a move which had raised not a few eyebrows and brought disgruntled comments from others within the rank and file of the police. But now, after being drafted in this morning, Williams looked across and caught Morthouse glancing behind to see what was happening and followed his gaze inside the house,

"I'm just thankful it was not me who was trusted with this assignment. Look out, here comes Fowler again…." A small whippet-like man with a thunderous face came storming past them out of the house and the very movement of him down the stairs and onto the pavement made the crowd of onlookers take an instinctive step back, as if a tiger had been loosed from within its cage and released amongst them. He glared up the street, taking out his pocket watch to check the time and then with a sharp about turn strode back into the house, not before casting Morthouse a poisonous glare. "…oh yes," added Williams, "very thankful indeed."

"I am glad that my predicament brings you so much relief," replied Morthouse, "this is the last thing which I would wish given my dressing down from McAllister not a week ago.

Sergeant McAllister was the direct reporting line for the constables and a person with whom they would wish to have no contact unless it was completely unavoidable. He was a heavy set man with wiry whiskers down his cheeks and his face had a weathered look which indicated many a long night out in the cold winters of Edinburgh. Indeed, if the Edinburgh police were to issue a notice to show the face of experienced policing, then Morthouse imagined that the face of Sergeant McAllister would be that very one. After the incident with

the theft, Morthouse had been summonsed to the office of Sergeant McAllister and had been subjected to the ranting of a man in full flight with his anger.
Morthouse had stiffened his body and was determined to hold his posture despite the musty breath in his face and the uncompromising look in Sergeant McAllister's eyes. He was determined to hold firm and would not allow himself to blink or cringe and give his Sergeant the satisfaction he was craving. "I'm waiting for an explanation, Morthouse," the words spat forcefully out at him again.
"Sir, there were four men up against only myself and Constable Williams and at least two of them were armed with cudgels. We gave chase down Fleshmarket Close from the High Street and at that point they turned to face us and blocked us in at the back. We had no option but to try to defend ourselves with our nightsticks but they were upon us too quickly. We fought with them until we could secure an escape back to the High Street and summon assistance. Then...."
"Then, as I understand it, you let them all escape! Not only did they steal alcohol and money from a public house and cause damage to the property but you let them escape when you had them almost in hand. Is that not correct?" Morthouse shook his head, starting to fluster at the bombardment he was receiving,
"No, sir, it was they who had us cornered. We could not despatch four of them when there were only the two of us...."
The Sergeant cut him off before he could go any further,
"A poor excuse, you are wearing the uniform of the Edinburgh City Police and this is the best that you can carry out your duties? You may only have been in the job for a few

weeks, son, but you had better pick yourself up by your bootstraps and sharpen up or you will be back running errands for your brother before you know it." Morthouse had felt his hackles rise but he knew it would be to his detriment to vent any reaction to this so he submitted to a few more minutes of ear bashing before being dismissed, leaving the room to return to his duties. He had not expected it to be easy but since he had started it felt like an uphill slog every day with the long hours and lack of sleep taking their toll on his body. For the first time he had begun to wonder if he had done the right thing in leaving his studies to join the Police. Despite coming from a well-to-do background he was not a weak individual but his constitution was being severely tested, not to mention his strength of character. The one thing that would hold him steady on his course was the need within him to prove his brother wrong and more than that to step out from the shadow of his father.

James Morthouse's father had been the well respected Edinburgh lawyer William Morthouse whose sudden demise had thrown the long standing family business into some disarray. The firm of Morthouse and Morthouse had been in Edinburgh for three generations of the Morthouse family and it was the certain intention of William Morthouse that his two sons would follow in his footsteps. 'There are two names above the door,' he would say to both brothers, 'and you must earn your right to have one of them.' It was only by the good fortune of being five years older that Morthouse's brother, Andrew, had been the first to lay claim to one of those titular names and in doing so had cemented James mind to deviate on to another path in life. The pressures which mounted upon James Morthouse to follow in his brothers footsteps and look to secure the other moniker in the business name had been great but in the final event it was the sudden death of their father which had released James from his studies and from his obligation. His father's death had been a sudden and tragic moment which had sent shockwaves through the family and at that same moment had elevated Andrew Morthouse to senior partner in the business. It had been the case for some time that in order to supplement his studies, James had been assisting his father in the business in small ways to gain access to the working knowledge of the business but his brother, clearly embracing his newly acquired promotion, saw his younger brother as a subordinate who would be best suited to the work of a clerk rather than an aspiring lawyer, which set them apart from any possibility of a continuation of the family business. After a heated discussion on the matter over the Christmas dinner table, and the New Year bringing to a focus the future direction for all concerned it was agreed that James would pursue his ambition to join the Edinburgh Police while leaving the business for Andrew who in due turn would hope one day to marry and have a son of his own who could take up the vacant desk in the office.

So it was that now, on the 22nd day of March 1882, James Morthouse found himself standing on the front steps of the home of Mr and Mrs Arthur Turner watching a coffin being carried in to the house to collect its cargo. The small crowd that had gathered in the street craned their necks to try and see what was going on inside the house and wondered who the unlucky tenant of the wooden box being loaded inside

would be. It was hardly surprising that there was a curiosity amongst the neighbours as it was impossible not to have noticed that some strange events had been taking place. This was in addition to the fact that a police constable had been present at the house almost continuously for over three weeks, that being Constable Morthouse. From where Morthouse stood on the front steps with Williams, thus positioned to carry out the dual function of keeping the crowd back from the door but also staying out of the way of Detective Fowler inside, he could hear raised voices which in some moments were bordering on hysterical. Just then, Detective Fowler exited the house and fixed Morthouse with a dark stare, his foul temperament easily discernable. Detective Fowler barked for Williams to go inside and do something more useful and then, surveying the watching crowd decided that they were not enough of a deterrent to defer the words he wished to have with Constable Morthouse,
"What have you been doing this past three weeks Morthouse? This should have been cleared up long ago but no, now we find ourselves with a dead body on our hands!" He thrust the small notebook in his hand towards Morthouse's face, "I'm not writing up a glowing account of your progress here Morthouse so you had better come up with some answers." Morthouse was under no illusion that he would be getting any praise from Fowler,
"I appreciate your anger sir, but this is not as simple as everyone perceives. I have been on watch each night but have been unable to apprehend any person carrying out the disturbances. They seem to be unfathomable." Fowler was about to respond when his eyes darted further up the road towards a hansom which had come to a sudden stop.

Morthouse looked around in the same direction and saw three men alight from the cab and stand watching. Fowler let out some mutterings of disgust just as a clatter from inside disrupted him and he marched back into the house to see what was happening. Morthouse could well imagine how this would look on his part and it made him agitated to think that he would be getting the blame for this situation. Yes, the case was not resolved but had anyone come to his assistance these past weeks when he had made them aware of the difficulty? No, they had not, but now they would be presumptuous enough to cast the eye of blame in his direction. Fowler appeared again at the top of the steps,
"Morthouse! Get these people moved back so we can bring the coffin to the wagon." Morthouse busied himself to the task but again could hear Fowler muttering under his breath, "Holmes, hah, no need for amateurs here," he muttered and he straightened his body and stared defiantly in the direction of the three men at the hansom as if to show that he had the situation well in hand. Morthouse could see the men only in glances through the crowd of onlookers but one of them had looked familiar to him. Sherlock Holmes was not well known in the public circles but reports of his involvement with Scotland Yard had travelled in tales passed through the police and Morthouse was aware of him, his likeness having been reproduced by an artist in London and distributed to make those aware who may come across him. Why was he here in Edinburgh at this time? Morthouse kept pressing the crowd back, much to their annoyance and protestations and the two undertakers men brought out the coffin and pushed it unceremoniously into the hearse. Morthouse was about to remind them of their duty to respect the dead when Mrs.

Victoria Turner appeared in the doorway watching the coffin being removed. She was weeping fearfully into her handkerchief as the men mounted the hearse and Fowler gave them their instructions before turning back,
"Morthouse! I shall avail myself of a ride with these men and we shall take this matter up later, rest assured we will!" He hauled himself onto the front of the hearse and with a shake of the reins the horses trotted forward removing the body from the scene. The main excitement having passed the crowd began to slowly disperse and Morthouse caught sight further up the street of the hansom's door being opened and the men proceeding back inside. The maid who was standing next to Mrs. Turner in the doorway distracted him for a moment,
"Come now m'lady, you should come back inside," she gestured and guided Mrs. Turner back indoors with a gentle hand. Morthouse walked slowly back up the steps to follow them in, the tiredness he had been fending off suddenly striking him at this moment. He stopped and turned to look up the street again and was astounded to see the man he had identified as Sherlock Holmes looking directly at him, one foot on the step in to the hansom. Morthouse turned fully and looked back and saw the man tip his hat and replace it again before climbing the step into the hansom as it then rattled off in the direction it had been travelling. Morthouse could not help but wonder what the supposed great detective would make of their situation here but put the notion out of his head as he walked back into the house, closing the door firmly behind him.

Chapter 7

The atmosphere in the house was now frantic as the servants engaged themselves in trying to console Mrs Turner, and Mr. Turner was prowling around the entrance hall like an animal about to charge, which in truth was not far from being the case. He turned and saw Morthouse standing just inside the front door, "Come with me..." he said, more quietly and deliberately than Morthouse was expecting which only gave him cause to be more concerned. Mr Turner walked into his study and stood holding the door, glaring at Morthouse and continuing to do so until he had walked past into the room when the door was slammed closed behind him. Mr. Turner paced quickly around in front of him and stood only a few feet in front of Morthouse, his face turning red and his eyes blazing,

"What are you going to do now?" he shouted, "you have been here long enough to resolve this matter but instead we find ourselves with a death on our hands. I demand an explanation and some reassurance that you have this in hand before someone else befalls an unfortunate fate?" Since joining the police Morthouse, for his part, had become accustomed to such outbursts directed towards him and remained resolutely calm.

"Sir, I appreciate your concern but I am trying to carry out my job with limited resources. In spite of even that this case would seem to be of a particularly unusual nature and may take some time to fathom." The reasoning held no water with Mr. Turner,

"I can appreciate that the matter may be somewhat removed from your usual cases but I pay my taxes and I wish to have results! When will your Detective Fowler return to assist with the investigation?" Morthouse in fact had no idea if Fowler was even returning to the scene since it seemed that he was being left here to stew in his own juices. This, he presumed, was no doubt Sergeant McAllister remaining true to his word and trying to hang him out to dry like so many clothes dangling above the closes of the old town.

"I am sure he will return presently but in the meantime I must make use of the time to carry out some investigation of my own so if you will excuse me, Mr Turner." Morthouse gave a nod of his head and was turning to leave the room but Mr. Turner would not let the matter rest,

"Aah, yes, thank goodness for that – Constable Morthouse is on the case and we can all rest easy. We will know the progress you are making when we find another body on our staircase, shall we?" Morthouse spun around, his patience now having expired, and was about to retort when the study door opened and Mrs Turner entered, preventing Morthouse the satisfaction to respond. Her cheeks were stained with tears but she had regained some composure and closed the door quietly behind her, her expression seemingly admonishing both her husband and Morthouse.

"What on earth is going on here," she whispered loudly, "everyone can hear you and this is not helping to calm the rest of the house. The staff are already unsettled as you can imagine and we should set them an example by which they can be reassured. If we can not even do this in private then we should at the very least make sure that it does not show in public. What good will come from this uproar? Arthur you must apologise to Constable Morthouse, he is clearly trying

to do his job and it will not help matters to turn on him now."
Mr. Turner let out a sharp laugh,
"Ha! I will not apologise and if I have offended Mr. Morthouse here, and I withhold his professional title most assuredly, then I am glad of it. Perhaps it will spur him into some productive endeavour." Morthouse did not rise to the bait, believing correctly that in this circumstance the higher ground was the better place to be positioned,
"Mrs Turner, thank-you for your support and rest assured that I will put every effort into bringing this matter to a conclusion. I can imagine the distress this is causing to both you and your husband and I shall double my work." She smiled sympathetically,
"I am sure you will, however like my husband, I should like a swift conclusion to our trials here. My nerves have been wrought enough with the activity these past weeks as it was and now we must endure the discovery of our lodger in such a way that is most upsetting, not to mention that we are a private family and do not wish the gaze of Edinburgh upon us. I am curious as to the whereabouts of Detective Fowler at the moment, should he not be present to assist?" Morthouse suppressed the answer he should like to have given,
"I am sure he will return soon, Mrs. Turner. He may be making enquiries elsewhere.
"But why would he make enquiries elsewhere when everything happened here? I would suggest that there is something going on here to which we are not privy and it does not rest easy with me. Is there anyone else that you may call on to assist?" Morthouse hesitated for only a second but it was very quickly picked up by Mrs. Turner, "Constable Morthouse? You know of someone?" He felt uneasy with this

but maybe one should not fly in the face of what fate had made apparent to you,
"Not that I can suggest from my colleagues in the police, but I became aware this morning of one man who may be able to help us although I am uncertain in what way." He paused as he was met with looks of confusion and enquiry from the two other parties in the room,
"The name of this person is…?" Mrs Turner asked.
"His name is Sherlock Holmes," Morthouse continued, "he is usually resident in London but by some strange coincidence I saw him this very morning as I was outside maintaining the order of the crowd which had gathered. As I stood, a carriage stopped a short distance away and three men came out and were clearly curious as to what was happening here. I recognised one of those gentlemen as Sherlock Holmes, I have seen his likeness and he is not someone whose identity is easily mistaken." Mrs Turner looked none the wiser as to how this person would be of assistance and Mr. Turner had resumed to pacing back and forth across the study,
"This man, what does he do exactly?" Mrs Turner asked, "If he is not in the police then how can he help us? Is he a spiritualist?"
"No madam, I believe he makes himself available as a private consulting detective. I have had no dealings with him and I have no knowledge on his methods but I have heard some rumblings from colleagues that he has helped Scotland Yard on a few occasions now."
"Scotland Yard, indeed?" Mrs. Turner asked.
"Yes, in London. From my understanding when they are no longer making progress on a case then they may request his

assistance." Mr. Turner threw his arms up in a mocking gesture,
"Wonderful, that is just the assistance we need. Do we not have enough amateurs on our case already without bringing in one more? No, we have engaged our police to handle this and handle it they should." Mrs. Turner walked over and put a hand on his arm,
"Let us not be too hasty here Arthur. Perhaps it would be of some benefit to have a fresh perspective on this situation. I suggest that we at least meet with this Sherlock Holmes first to see what he can offer?" Mr Turner again protested,
"Absolutely not, I forbid any contact with this man, do you hear? For good or ill, and in my estimation usually the latter, we have our police and we shall not bring in strangers to our situation. That is my final word!" With this proclamation he held up his hand towards his wife to prevent any reply and marched resolutely from the room.
Morthouse watched him go and then turned back to Mrs Turner who was watching after her husband who, it would be wondered, did not feel the piercing stare strike him between the shoulder blades and bring him to the floor. She turned towards Morthouse and gave a small, polite smile which was clearly ready on her lips from past experience,
"Constable Morthouse, please accept my apologies. My husband can on occasion be taken to irrational temper." Morthouse dropped his eyes,
"Please, no need to explain, Mrs Turner. I hope he will calm down soon enough?" She cocked her head to one side thoughtfully,
"He may, he may, however I believe that the one thing that may ensure this is if we are no longer under the cloud of our

current problem, and I believe we should explore all avenues available, do you not agree?" She paused momentarily, "Constable Morthouse would you please arrange to contact this, Mr. Holmes, was it? How do we locate him in Edinburgh?"

Morthouse looked uneasy at this suggestion and his concern was clearly evident in his expression, "What is the matter?" she asked him.

"Mrs. Turner, it is not within my authority to bring Mr. Holmes in on this case. I am a constable and it would take the approval of my superiors, most likely Detective Fowler, to engage him and I would not expect that authority will be given."

"May I ask why not?" she said.

"If I may speak frankly, and in confidence madam," he paused while she nodded and gestured for him to continue, "the police will not engage Mr. Holmes as to do so would be to admit that they can make no further progress. As I say I am not in possession of the full facts but as I understand the police in London have thus far managed to keep his involvement with them secret and out of the papers. London is a large city but I would fear that in a smaller city such as Edinburgh, and given the focus on the house, that his involvement would not be kept secret. I could not recommend a course of action that would cause embarrassment for the police or my superiors." Mrs Turner looked perplexed and her face darkened,

"So you are saying we should not make use of him?" Morthouse shifted uneasily,

"No, Mrs. Turner. I am saying that I can not request his services..." He paused again hoping that his truncated

statement would make the next part obvious but she did not pick up on this subtlety so he continued, "….but if you were to engage him directly then it would obviously be outside of my control to prevent you from doing so." She smiled now,
"Indeed. Then I have come to this decision under my own steam and will therefore engage the services if I can of Mr. Sherlock Holmes." Morthouse was torn now as he had effectively admitted defeat in this case but what was he to do? After only a short time in this job he had been abandoned to his fate in what was clearly an attempt to give him enough rope to hang himself. If Sergeant McAllister and Detective Fowler wished to make sport of him then he would return the compliment and in this way he was not to blame for Mrs. Turner's decision to seek outside help, providing that is that they continued to respect his confidence. "How can I find this man, Constable Morthouse? I assume he has taken lodging with someone during his stay?"
"I am not aware of where he is staying but I believe I have the means to find out. One of the gentlemen that was with him was a Doctor Patrick Watson, I know him from when my father died as he performed a post mortem to determine the cause of his death. I know where he lives in town and I suggest if you were to start there, then he would most likely be able to point you in the right direction towards his lodgings."
"Us," she said. Morthouse looked puzzled, "Us, Constable Morthouse. He will point us in the direction of Mr. Holmes."
"But I can not play any part in this Mrs. Turner, as I explained…." She stopped him with a hand held up in front of her,

“You have been pressured into this by me and I have asked you to ensure my safety. Besides, I will need you to bring this Mr. Holmes up to date with your findings so far, such as they are, but I will take responsibility for bringing him into my house. If Detective Fowler wishes to take issue with me over this then he may do so.” She walked to the study door and opened it wide, “I suggest we make headway on this matter first thing tomorrow morning, I feel it may be more easily achieved if we wait until my husband has returned to work and is safely out of our way at the bank.

Chapter 8

The following morning Morthouse watched from the upper landing as Mr. Turner departed at eight o'clock to return to his work. It seemed slightly incongruous to him that after such an event had taken place as happened yesterday that he should be so ready to put it behind him, however it was the case that people handled such situations in their own way. He also guessed that in the matter of running a bank, as was Mr. Turner's profession, the priority to tend for the money therein overtook many of the other usual considerations. The household otherwise was still in a state of shock and the staff had a tired, pallid look to them which belied their attempts to return to normality. Mrs. Turner appeared promptly in the entrance hallway at nine o'clock and Morthouse joined her before going outside to hail a hansom for the journey to Charlotte Square.

The cab ride to Patrick Watson's house was brief but provided Morthouse with really his first chance to observe Mrs. Turner in close quarters. Thus far in his attendance at their house she had kept her distance and was reluctant to become involved, preferring to leave her husband to deal with him, but now that the situation had taken a more dramatic turn she had seemed to accept it as a call to action. He mused that it seemed often the case that although it was Mr. Turner who would gee up the horses it was often Victoria Turner who would steer the carriage so to speak. For the first time he noticed that underneath the lines of worry which seemed to have constantly crossed her brow these past weeks that she was a person with a gentle face but in character she had a strength which was thankfully tempered with a kind heart. He knew of enough people of strong character who were found to be highly disagreeable, if not arrogant or obnoxious, due to their lacking one of the finer character traits to provide a counterpoint in their nature. It was indeed fortunate that Mrs. Turner was not one of these latter types and would now seem to be turning a corner from her position as helpless victim into one who would seek out a way forward.

They spoke little during the journey other than to exchange small pleasantries on the weather and the current Edinburgh gossip which was a currency in much demand in the city. Morthouse tried to keep his observances of their fellow citizens light and away from crime as the further that they travelled from the house the lighter the burden seemed on Mrs. Turner. She seemed, not to forget the problems she was experiencing with the terrible business at home, but to leave them behind for a moment. Her expression was still laced with worry and tiredness and no small journey would remove the memory of yesterday's events but at least for a brief period they seemed to be somewhere else rather than enclosing her on all sides.

The four wheeler came to a stop outside their destination and as they disembarked to the pavement Morthouse was not certain but he thought he had seen a curtain twitch slightly in the front window. Mrs. Turner did not hesitate and to ensure that for any casual observer who would care to note it, it was she who was taking the lead in this matter. Morthouse remained a step behind to allow her to pull the bell beside the front door. Moments later the door was opened and a young

housemaid stood before them, “Good morning, may I help you?”
“I hope so,” Mrs. Turner replied, “we are hoping to speak to Doctor Watson if he is available?”
“Which one?” came the response.
“I beg your pardon? I believe this is the home of Doctor Patrick Watson, I was not aware another of the same name lived here?” The housemaid opened the door wide,
“Come in if you please ma’am, my apologies. I will fetch Doctor Watson for you.” She disappeared into a door off the hallway and they could hear her speak with a gentleman, who then appeared with the housemaid following behind,
“Thank-you Jessie,” he said, allowing the maid to retire, “I am Patrick Watson, how may I be of assistance.” Mrs. Turner smiled warmly and held out her hand which he shook,
“Forgive us for intruding on you so early Doctor Watson, my name is Victoria Turner and this is Constable Morthouse….” She was about to continue but a look of recognition came across Doctor Watson’s face,
“Excuse me for asking but are you the wife of Arthur Turner, resident of Heriot Row?”
“Indeed I am, I can see that you are probably aware of our situation.” Doctor Watson nodded, slightly embarrassed, “well, I am hoping that you may be able to help us Doctor.”
“I would of course, if I can but I am uncertain how I may be of assistance. By chance we were passing your house yesterday morning and noticed that there had been some further, and I would venture more serious, incident but….”
“Exactly,” she said before pausing, her voice trembling slightly now as the memory returned and made more clear the reason for their current visit, “and it is with this that you can

hopefully help us. This young man has been posted to our house and he saw you outside the house yesterday morning. He informs me that he recognised one of your companions, a Mr. Sherlock Holmes we believe?" Patrick nodded slowly,
"Yes, he was with me, as was his friend and my cousin Doctor John Watson." It was the turn of Mrs. Turner and Morthouse to exchange a quick glance, making sense now of the remark of the maid,
"We would like to find this Mr. Holmes and we thought that you may be able to point us in the direction of his lodgings? I know it is most unusual that you should do so but I would be most grateful."
"I can certainly do that, with no hesitation Mrs. Turner since I know that it will be for no foul nature that you wish to see him. I can take you to him right away." She looked reassured,
"Then we were correct to come to you, thank-you. We have a cab waiting outside if you would wish to accompany us or if you can tell us the address where he is staying in Edinburgh?" Patrick waved a hand,
"No need, he is right here in my house. I can show you into him right now. Please wait here for a moment and I can check if he is available." They watched, somewhat stunned at their good fortune, as he walked over to a door leading from the entrance hall and opened it, taking a step inside, "Mr. Holmes," they heard him say, "it seems you have visitors."

Shortly after, two gentlemen followed Patrick out into the reception hall, one of whom smiled warmly and held out his hand to each of them, "Mrs Turner, Constable Morthouse, permit me to introduce myself, I am John Watson, Patrick's cousin."

“I gather you are also a doctor, is that correct?” Mrs. Turner asked.
“Indeed, although I would add not quite so distinguished a one as my cousin. This gentleman here,” he now said gesturing to the other man “is Mr. Sherlock Holmes.” Both Mrs. Turner and Morthouse smiled and nodded their heads to the man who came forward to shake their hands but he was not as effusive as the other two gentlemen they had just met. Morthouse observed his steely grey eyes set into his thin hawk like face and wondered just what kind of a man it was that they would now be dealing.
“I am very pleased to meet you,” Holmes said in his usual cool manner, “pray tell me, how did you come to find me here? My visit to Edinburgh was at the last minute and I was not aware my lodgings would be common knowledge in the town?” Mrs Turner laughed slightly,
“Well Mr. Holmes, I think you may find that word can travel very fast indeed through the sculleries and kitchens of Edinburgh. There is nothing which remains a secret very long here once it has left your own lips. In fact I sometimes wonder if gossip must even do that before it is whisking its way to the ears of strangers. But in this instance I must credit Constable Morthouse with this information.” Holmes turned his gaze towards Morthouse and studied him,
“Indeed. Then I must congratulate Constable Morthouse but in doing so can you tell me how you tracked me down?” Morthouse straightened his posture as if ready to give a statement in a court of law,
“It was nothing really, Mr. Holmes. I saw you yesterday morning in the street outside Mrs. Turner’s house and I recognised not only you but also Doctor Watson,” he stopped

briefly looking at the two doctors, “I mean, that is to say Doctor Patrick Watson, who I am sure will not remember, but he carried out the post mortem on my father some months back.” Patrick registered a look of understanding on his face,
“Yes, yes, of course. Morthouse, I knew the name was familiar to me but I could not place it. I remember the matter, a sad case indeed, very perplexing if I recall.” Morthouse nodded in deference to this,
“Thank-you sir. Once I had recognised Doctor Watson then it seemed a logical place to start our enquiry since you were clearly an acquaintance of the doctor.” Holmes clapped his hands suddenly,
“Hah! Excellent young Constable Morthouse,” his sudden outburst startling all nearby since he had until this point taken on the composure of a statue, “a small point on which you picked up, although I did linger long enough at the carriage to ensure you had spotted me. Two things I find interesting here, Watson, will you enlighten us?” The other Doctor Watson looked put upon as if being asked to perform,
“Well Holmes, clearly the young man was able to recognise you this morning which suggests he is well read as I don’t believe you are very well known outside of London. Secondly that he has a gift for observation and intuition.”
“Exactly, thank-you Watson. It was a small feat to come to our door but it gives me some heart that despite your age you have an eye to observe and that is key in the business you have chosen. Now, I can only presume that you have come to discuss with me the events occurring at your house, Doctor Watson is there somewhere that we could utilise for our consultation?” Patrick nodded,

"Of course, this way," he led them down the hallway and off into a sizeable study the walls of which were lined with bookcases of medical notes and text books which reminded Morthouse of his father's office. The walls were adorned with beautiful oak panelling and in one corner a consulting desk sat across the room and Holmes seemed to almost dance around it and then gesture them into the two chairs in front,
"Please, be seated," he said.
Patrick looked at his pocket watch, "John, we should really go." Watson nodded but looked slightly ill at ease, turning back to face Holmes and smiling, his eyebrow raised enquiringly,
"Would you like me to stay Holmes?" he asked.
"No need Watson," he replied with a wave of his hand, "I believe I have this all under control. Besides which I would not wish you to miss your outing today on my account. I shall no doubt catch up with you later in the day." He smiled at Watson and sat down behind the desk, his elbows resting on the arms of the chair and his hands in front of his face, fingertips pressed together. Once the other two gentlemen had left the room, Holmes looked at Mrs. Turner and Morthouse, "Now, as you may be aware my time in Edinburgh is limited, therefore if I can ask you for a brief summary of the events thus far then I can determine if I may assist. I'm afraid we have no time to waste at the moment on the smallest details, those can come later."
"I believe I shall let Constable Morthouse relay the facts, Mr. Holmes," Mrs. Turner replied, "as I fear that I may not be fully aware of all of the circumstances since given my direct involvement in the matter I may be too close to it all to see it clearly. Constable, if you would be so kind?" Holmes nodded

and turned his gaze to Morthouse who felt slightly unnerved with the intensity of the enquiry now focused upon him. He took out a small tattered notebook from his jacket pocket and opened it to the first page and was about to speak when Holmes interjected,

"I pray remind you Constable Morthouse, only the main facts if you please. I do not wish to hear your testimony word for word from what is, I am sure, a detailed transcription in your notebook. We are not in the court, and I am not the jury although that is not to say I shall not reach a judgement." Holmes smiled, "Please, continue…" Morthouse folded his notebook closed and laid it on his lap,

"As you wish Mr. Holmes. My involvement in the case started a few weeks ago when I was posted to the home of Mr. and Mrs. Turner to investigate the strange occurrences to which they had been subjected. Mrs. Turner had been the first to hear the noises I believe followed soon after by Mr. Turner."

"How would you describe these noises?" Holmes asked.

"They were thumps or bangs coming from downstairs at first, then on following nights they seemed to come from other areas of the house. These first nights were prior to my attendance at the house but I have found the disturbances to be very similar to how Mrs. Turner has described them." He stopped momentarily to gather his next thought but, despite her initial reluctance to describe the case, Mrs. Turner interjected,

"You see Mr. Holmes, I am a very light sleeper. I will often find myself awakened by the noise of the servants retiring and had done so that first night but this thudding noise was different. I had earlier heard the servants going to their rooms and the house being quiet I had dropped off to sleep but was awakened again by I did not know what. It was a simple knocking noise coming from downstairs and as I awoke fully and sat up to listen I could hear it in the direction of the parlour. Then it seemed to be moving through the hallway and then it faded. I woke my husband but he sleeps soundly and was only roused slightly and did not take any notice."

"Did you investigate the noise?"

"No, Mr. Holmes, although I found it odd at such a late hour I dismissed it as being someone moving around downstairs, perhaps our housemaid who had forgotten one of her duties and had risen to carry it out."

"You asked her the next morning I presume if she had been abroad in the night?"

"I did, but she assured me that she had turned in at around eleven o'clock and did not leave her room again until five thirty when she rose to start lighting the fires." Holmes nodded but did not say anything, merely gesturing her to continue as he closed his eyes. Mrs. Turner looked towards Morthouse, not quite sure if they had lost the attention of Holmes but this was soon clearly not the case as his voice rose impatiently, "Please Mrs. Turner, continue if you will, you have my fullest attention!"

"Well, the noise continued for the next few nights and I began to grow tired of the broken sleep each night. Arthur, my husband, was still convinced it was one of the servants and on the fifth night, wondering if they were up to no good, he went to check on the noise but when he did so the knocking stopped as quickly as it started. He went to the top of the stairs but no-one could be seen or heard." Holmes opened his eyes and looked at Mrs. Turner,

"I believe I can see the pattern of events which had been started and I need hear no more now of that part of your tale. I would be grateful if you could move forward until we have the involvement of the police." He continued to watch her now, every so often flicking his gaze to Morthouse who was now sitting uncomfortably, feeling rather redundant.
"It was the following week," she continued, "that was when we had the first damage caused by the spirit." A flicker of some emotion crossed Holmes' face, unseen by his guests but if they had it was so well disguised they would not have recognised it as disdain. In Holmes' line of work he had heard many stories from people who should perhaps have better spent their time elsewhere, allowing Holmes to also spend his more fruitfully. "The noises began as always in the early hours of the morning, the usual rhythmic knocking growing progressively louder. Arthur and I were so tired with the constant disturbance night after night and I believe Arthur was feeling the lack of sleep most profoundly and it was starting to have an effect on his work."
"What does you husband do, Mrs. Turner?"
"He is in banking, he is a partner in a large bank in the city and a very successful and well respected institution in Edinburgh. When the noise started to become louder, Arthur sat bolt upright in bed and simply shouted for them to stop. He is not by nature one to start shouting…" this time it was Morthouse who allowed a brief flicker of incredulity to cross his face given the recent altercation with Mr. Turner and it was not unnoticed by Holmes. "…however," she continued, "the strain was starting to be felt by both of us. It was then that we heard a loud crash against our bedroom door. I let out a scream and would not come out from under our bedclothes

but Arthur went to investigate, as did the rest of the household who had been awakened by the noise, and he found that a large vase which had been on a table at the bottom of the stairs had been smashed against the door. But again we could see no evidence of any human hand behind our haunting."
"You questioned the servants again but to no avail I presume?"
"We did, Mr. Holmes and in fact they were becoming frightened by the whole business."
"It was at this point that I assume you contacted the police?"
"Yes. Arthur was reluctant at first as he did not feel it was a police matter but I insisted as my wits were thoroughly shaken by this latest episode however they were not particularly interested at first. We endured more nights of the hauntings and each time Arthur would go out of the bedroom to investigate, taking a stout cane with him, but he could find nothing." Holmes looked unmoved, his face a blank canvas,
"Have these hauntings, as you put them, have they occurred every night since?"
"No, only every few nights in the main but sometimes we have them on consecutive nights. I did think at first that we were to be spared any further episode but then a night or two later they would recommence even more loudly than before. We only found an ally in the police when Arthur was carrying out some work for the Chief Inspector who was willing to pull some levers, as Arthur put it, to get things moving. That was when we met Constable Morthouse for the first time." Holmes stood up from behind the desk and walked to the fireplace to take up his customary position leaning on the mantle,

“So we have Constable Morthouse, who I observe has made no progress in solving the mystery, but in fact now has a dead body on his hands, am I correct?” Morthouse shifted uneasily in his chair,

“I’m afraid so, Mr Holmes. You see I am only a few months into my career with the police and was posted to the Turners and left to my own devices.”

“You have no detective branch in Edinburgh? I thought I saw a detective with you outside the house yesterday morning?”

“We do Mr. Holmes but they have not given me any assistance and I have not been allowed to call in any help from my colleagues. The man you saw me with was Detective Fowler and to say he would be unhappy about my involving you in this matter would be an understatement.”

“But,” Mrs Turner added, “as we have agreed Constable Morthouse, it is I who has insisted you accompany me to speak to Mr. Holmes and you shall have no culpability in the matter.” Holmes lit a match and put it to his pipe,

“The identity of the victim was…?” Holmes asked.

“He was our lodger, Mr. Holmes, a nice gentleman by the name of Mr. Woodbridge.” Holmes normally steely eyes began to sparkle now owing to the possibility of at least some small diversion during his stay in Edinburgh, if a death could be classed as merely a diversion.

“Mrs. Turner, I am glad to say that I shall come and investigate further on this matter. I had believed that this was a simple case, and in some respects I still do, however with the recent tragedy it may yet prove interesting and I should like to put you at ease again in your own home. However, given the conduct of this Detective Fowler I also believe that Constable Morthouse here may be glad of some assistance even if it is not to be admitted. I am sure between us we can put the lethargy of your superiors to work against them!" Mrs. Turner stood, and although the feeling of happiness was beyond her at the moment she at least felt reassured that some progress had been made. The only look on the face of Constable Morthouse was that of worry and the feeling that, for him at least, his troubles were only about to increase.

Chapter 9

Sherlock Holmes alighted from the carriage outside the Turner's home and walked swiftly to the front door with Mrs. Turner and Morthouse following behind. As he reached the door he spun round to face them, holding up his hand and then drawing them in closer, "May I ask who is aware of your visit to me this morning?"

"No-one apart from Constable Morthouse and myself, Mr Holmes, – we told no-one else since we did not know if we would be able to find you."

"Can I infer from this that your husband is not a willing participant in my attending?"

"No, indeed, in fact he forbade me from seeking your help, however I believe he may not have been thinking very clearly. He has been under a great strain in his work of late and this has only compounded the matter. Why do you ask?"

Holmes pondered for a moment,

"I wish as few people as possible to know of my involvement, both for fear of the backlash which it may bring on Constable Morthouse from his superiors but also to allow me some time away from the glare of the police. I find that once my involvement in a case is known then my room to manoeuvre is often made more restrictive. May I suggest that when we speak to any of the household servants that you simply introduce me as Mr. Holmes and that I am a spiritualist from London who has heard of your predicament and has come to offer any assistance with your haunting." Mrs. Turner and Morthouse nodded in agreement, "Good, I will take care of the rest to convince them by my actions. Now, may I propose that we commence our investigation

proper? Please…" He stood aside and gestured towards the door to allow Mrs. Turner and Morthouse to enter the house while he followed after them in to the entrance hall. A young woman appeared as they closed the door and took their coats,
"Margaret," Victoria Turner asked, "is Mr. Turner in his study?"
"No ma'am, as he left this morning he asked me to tell you that he had some urgent business to attend to and he would return for supper." Mrs. Turner thanked her and sent her back to her duties,
"Where would you like to start Mr. Holmes?" Holmes glanced around the hallway and noted the expensive art on the walls and some fine pieces of furniture which would have cost a pretty penny to acquire. He found it unusual for one who is concerned with the business of the careful management of money and investment to put on display such flagrant spending. Holmes pointed towards the stairs, "If I may…." He did not wait for an answer but took the stairs two at a time and then stopped on the landing above, "which room belonged to your lodger?" Mrs Turner made to open the bedroom door in front of them but Holmes stepped in front of her,
"My apologies, but please allow me…." He stopped at the door and knelt down in front of it, his hands hovering over it and seeming to try to draw information out of it by some unknown divination. To those looking on, his actions seemed to fit in perfectly with his cover story of being a psychic however had Watson been present he would have been well used to Holmes unhindered methods of observation. He stood up again and put his hand to the doorknob, turning it slowly and pushing the door inwards to show a respectably sized

bedroom which looked to have been tidily kept by its occupant. “Has anyone been into this room, aside from the police of course? No maids or servants have set foot in here?” Morthouse shook his head,

“No, sir, none of them have any desire to do so either.” Holmes looked around the room, again his hands and eyes working in tandem from around the bed, along the floor and up and down the walls. He moved with such energy around the room, from flitting along the wall to lunging down towards the floor, and then back up again that Morthouse could not see how fruitful a result this would bring. “Mr. Holmes,” he said cautiously, “may I ask what you have found?” Holmes stood abruptly and put his hand to his mouth,

“I have not yet found anything which is conclusive in itself,” he replied sharply, “ but I have found certain things which may prove to be useful when I have concluded my investigation.” He turned away but then stopped and turned back towards Morthouse, “You have had the opportunity to examine this room I take it?”

“Yes, sir.”

“Tell me what you found from your investigation, I am curious to hear your views on the incident.” Morthouse took out his notebook again and flipped through the pages, at which Holmes sighed, “Constable, tell me what you have seen, what is you instinct, your feeling of the room and of the lodger from your observation?” Morthouse again closed his notebook,

“Well sir, to my eye, this was nothing but a terrible accident. It seems clear that Mr. Woodbridge came out of his room to try to find out the source of the noise during the night and,

being without a light, he stumbled and fell down the stairs. I would expect his neck to be broken or some such injury which proved the fatal blow." Holmes smiled thinly at him,
"You are correct that there was a fatal blow, but not in the respect I feel you may imagine. I would direct your attention to the dressing table here, and specifically now to the wall just inside the door. Tell me, Mrs Turner, how long is it since Mr. Woodbridge moved in to his lodgings here?"
"It was about a month ago, Mr Holmes. He was working for my husband, who was training him in the business, when his previous lodging fell through and he was in need of somewhere to stay. Arthur suggested that he might move in with us for a time and having met the young man I was inclined to concur since he was an agreeable gentleman."
"Was he aware of the problem you were having with the hauntings?" asked Holmes.
"He was, but he was also in need of somewhere to stay and since we had agreed that he need not pay us any rent for his room the terms were very favourable for him even with our disturbances." Holmes smiled,
"How did he and your husband get along, were they well suited as mentor and pupil?" Mrs. Turner looked saddened as she thought about this,
"We never had any children Mr. Holmes and I believe that Arthur grew to see George as the son he never had. They would spend many hours in the study discussing their work and I understand that he was a diligent and keen learner and a great help to my husband." As she said this, the front door slammed closed and they could hear footsteps and low but earnest voices in the hallway below but their words could not

be discerned. A voice echoed up to them, "Victoria? Are you there?" followed by footsteps ascending the stairs.
Mrs. Turner looked crestfallen, whispering, "Oh dear, my husband, this is not how I had wished for the first meeting with you to take place." All three of them had turned to face the stairway as if ready to meet an oncoming assailant,
"Victoria?" Arthur Turner said as he turned around on to the top landing to be greeted by his wife, the sheepish looking Morthouse and a stranger who was smiling but any warmth was belied by his cool, constant stare. "What is going on? Who is this gentleman?" There was a momentary pause as Mrs. Turner tried to find the words to explain their current situation but it was in fact Holmes who seized the moment,
"Mr. Turner, I presume? May I introduce myself – I am Mr. Sherlock Holmes, at your service." He held out his hand but Mr. Turner did not accept the cordial gesture,
"I do not believe, sir, that I know you although your name was mentioned to me yesterday, but we have not requested your services here, whatever they may be, and nor do we wish them." Then turning back towards the staircase and leaning over, he shouted, "Fowler! You should come up here now!" There was a flurry of footsteps on the stair and the small frame of Detective Fowler appeared in front of them.
"Well, well, this is an interesting party we have here. Mr. Holmes if I'm not mistaken?" Holmes nodded and effected a smile which was purely perfunctory, "And how do we come to find you so close to the scene of the crime?" Holmes looked at them both for a moment before speaking,
"My dear Mr. Turner, Detective Fowler, I must offer my sincere apologies for my intrusion. I was passing by the house yesterday when I saw the commotion and my host in

Edinburgh was kind enough to bring me up to speed with the, what shall we say, local gossip? My curiosity being so piqued, I called to the house a short while ago to ask if I may be of assistance." He gestured towards Mrs Turner, "Your good wife was most reluctant to let me inside, however, and it is to my shame, I persisted and wore her down so that I could look at the scene." Arthur Turner was about to remonstrate most strongly when Fowler gestured and he paused,
"If you will allow me Mr Turner. You, Mr. Holmes, are not welcome or required here and I thank you to keep your nose out of police business. You may be tolerated by your friends in the Yard but your kind of interference will not be tolerated here." He puffed himself up to display his feeling of superiority in the situation but Holmes smiled and easily deferred,
"I must offer my apologies to you all and I will take my leave. If my services are not required then I am very glad to hear it, and I will wish you all a pleasant day." He made for the stairs and was followed down by Fowler and Mr. Turner who both exchanged irate glances and by Mrs. Turner and Morthouse who were in the same measure baffled and disappointed. Morthouse especially could not fathom why there was such concern over this man whom it would appear was no better than himself at solving crime. They reached the front door which was promptly opened by Fowler and his thunderous face was focused intently on Holmes, who was not in the least intimidated and took his time fastening his coat before leaving,
"Mrs. Turner, Mr Turner," said Holmes, "my apologies for any distress I may have caused with my intrusion. Please be

assured you shall hear nothing further from me and I shall content myself with your fine city for the remainder of my stay." Mrs Turner nodded and smiled but said nothing, not wishing to risk implicating herself. Holmes looked through the door and back again, "I must say that the chill is definitely more noticeable here than in London, I imagine it can be very harsh on the health? I myself have had an infernal head cold which will not seem to release its grip on me. I can only hope that I have not brought any illness into your house"

"Indeed, Mr Holmes," Mrs Turner replied, "but please, no need for concern, my husband and I keep excellent health and we do not take colds too often."

"Then you have been spared any such colds recently?" Holmes enquired.

"Yes, both fine and as fit as fiddles," she replied. Fowler's face was becoming increasingly grim and Holmes gave him a brief glance before turning to leave,

"I am very glad to hear of it, Mrs Turner, very glad. Now, I bid you farewell."

Chapter 10

Holmes stepped down on to the pavement and heard the door slam firmly behind him. His calculating eyes narrowed and an almost imperceptible smile appeared on his mouth as he turned and faced the building. It was a well appointed house and obviously inhabited by wealthy owners, and there was nothing to suggest to the casual observer of anything untoward taking place here. However, as he was inclined to point out to Watson on occasion, he was far from being merely a casual observer. He walked to the side of the house and, bending over for closer inspection, inspected the pathway around the house before reaching the back of the property where he stood straight and gave a satisfied smile to himself. Returning to the front of the house he glanced each way along the street spotting a small group of children, perhaps ten or eleven years old, playing a few hundred yards away. With a swift flick of his cane he set off in their direction, waiting until he was in easy earshot, "You boys, how would you like to earn a shilling a piece?" Their initial start was quickly dispelled with curiosity by the smiling stranger who had offered them such a sum which for them was a handsome reward whatever the task.

"What do we need to dae for it Mister?" came the response from a tousled and dirty young boy who was clearly nominated as leader of the small group. Holmes crouched down to meet them on the level,

"I shall give you a piece of paper my good man and I wish you to deliver it to a policeman for me." Their faces all looked startled,

"Och no, we're no having anything to do with the bobbies, he'll whack us with his stick."
"Not if you follow my instructions exactly, now listen to me"
They gathered around, intrigued and wary in equal measure as Holmes spoke to them but through his well earned experience of dealing with such street ruffians he gained their agreement on the bargain. He wrote and handed them a small note, the delivery of which was of little financial consequence to the detective but of notable value to the young incumbents. The matter could have been forsaken by Holmes for the time being as he was sure that his young charges would carry out his bidding, but with time to kill he settled himself into a lane someway up the street from the Turners house and watched patiently for any movement.

The afternoon was fine and clear and with his coat securely fastened against the chilling breeze, Holmes held his vigil over the street. This road, like the rest of the New Town, was designed with such majesty that it was impossible not to be impressed by the grandeur of the homes on display. Holmes was well accustomed to the finer areas of London as he was favoured to be in some demand amongst the more wealthy inhabitants of the city, and if he been one to consider such notions he would acknowledge that he felt comfortable and at home in Edinburgh, almost as if he had visited before if not in this but in a previous life. However, he was not one to give any thought to these feelings and was also wise enough to know that such buildings provided merely a uniform veneer of respectability to all cities whether it was the expanding metropolis of London or the learned city of Edinburgh. In each of the homes there were people of the same kind as in any other place and behind their doors must surely hide many dark secrets, which was indeed fortunate in being able to keep the mind of Sherlock Holmes occupied and his pocketbook nourished. It took some time longer than he had anticipated for any movement at the Turner's house but as happens many times in life, patience is rewarded. The door was opened and the detective, Fowler, stepped out and turned to shake hands with Mr. Turner who was clearly carrying an expression of some relief. They spoke for a moment, briefly stopping while Fowler hailed a passing hansom, and then the door was closed and Fowler departed in his cab. A few minutes afterwards the door was opened again and a crestfallen and weary-looking Constable Morthouse appeared, and it did not take too clever a deduction to know that this was clearly down to having been given a severe dressing down by his superior. Holmes watched as the young man walked down the steps and looked left and then right, his course of action not clear to him. Such indecision was not in Holmes' lexicon but he could sympathise with the position in which this young and inexperienced man had been placed. It was also apparent to Holmes however that what would follow should put him on some form of surer footing. Morthouse's hesitation was dispelled a moment later when the group of children came barrelling towards him and surrounded him, shouting and yelling and causing some disruption to his person. He yelled at them to be off, his tone of voice exposing his harassed state of mind, but as they gave a final yowl of protest Holmes saw one of the boys thrust the piece of paper into Morthouse's hand as they all the fled down the street being chased for a few paces by the constable who then registered the article now in his hand and stopped to examine the document. Taking a few moments to read the note, he folded it and placed it into his tunic pocket before returning to the house and disappearing inside.

Thus content that there was nothing further to be gained from this location at present, and with the persistent devil of time marching quickly forward, Holmes left his concealment and proceeded to trace the directions he had been given to the home of Dr. Joseph Bell. His stride was positive and his mood light as he recalled his encounter with detective Fowler and, as unavoidably dictated by the more mischievous streak in his character, he looked forward to having some compensation for his harsh treatment in the Turner house. It was a foolish man who would drift off to sleep at night finding comfort in the supposed knowledge that they had bested Sherlock Holmes. The walk to Dr. Bells was brief but despite his feeling of familiarity with the vista of Edinburgh it was no substitute for the in-depth knowledge he lacked of the place. In London he knew every street and lane and which of those to avoid and which may prove useful in his work but here, as the cold night started to drift in and the light was fading, he was blind to what lay around him other than what his current sightline could provide him in the way of intelligence.

The home of Joseph Bell was in Melville Street and was a fine Georgian town house indistinguishable from its neighbours and giving no indication of the distinguished resident. Holmes pressed the bell and the door was opened a few moments later by what seemed to be the housekeeper, being a woman in her sixties who carried herself with the air of someone who is comfortably in charge of their domain. "Yes, Mr. Holmes, we have been expecting you. You are the last to arrive and Dr. Bell has asked me to show you straight through." She led Holmes along the hallway and opened the door to a dining room splendidly laid out for their evening's repast. Three men turned to greet Holmes as he entered,

"Aah, Holmes," said Watson, "glad you could join us. Let me introduce you to Dr. Joseph Bell." Before Watson could turn to carry out the introduction a thin man with white hair and striking features walked purposefully forward and held out his hand,

"Mr. Holmes, I am pleased to finally make your acquaintance. I am Joseph Bell." Holmes shook hands and for the briefest moment they both seemed to be sizing the other up. The glances were brief but for each of those men the information which each seemed to gain of their counterpart was manifest. For any uninformed bystander who was fortunate enough to be watching the meeting they would not have been surprised to learn that these two gentlemen were long lost brothers such were the similarities in their appearance and in their manner. Dr. Bell was also possessed of the same sharp, piercing eyes but his were further up the spectrum of warmth than those of Holmes. His hair was the colour of iron having turned grey overnight during three days of intense mourning for his beloved wife Edith, who had died some years previously, having succumbed to the common but deadly peritonitis.

"Doctor Bell, it is a pleasure," Holmes replied warmly, "I have heard much about you from the doctors Watson here

and I have been looking forward to this evening very much."
Bell laughed,
"Indeed, I can think of no better moniker for our friends here than the doctors Watson," John and Patrick looked at each other with a raised eyebrow but took it in good humour, "we should perhaps look to ask them to perform a skit for us after dinner. My good man, I must also confess that I have heard something of your work and it is a delight to welcome you to my home. I feel we may have much to talk about this evening. Come, let us sit down and toast our gathering. I see you have walked here this evening, enjoying the New Town streets?" Holmes was about to enquire how he had known this but stopped short, recalling his conversation with Watson back in London,
"I have indeed, I see your observation is every bit as keen as your reputation had suggested. You notice the dirt upon my shoes no doubt?" Joseph Bell smiled and nodded,
"I did, nothing could be more certain. But enough of my parlour trick as I fear that you shall be more than a match for me in that regard. Now, let us dine…."

As was to be expected the meal was a most pleasant affair and the conversation was as wide ranging as one would expect from such a congregation. Joseph Bell related details of a case only the previous week, which had been christened in the press as the Argyleshire Murder, for which he had been called as an expert witness for the defence. "A very complex affair however I am glad to say that the man was found not guilty. It would clearly have been a miscarriage of justice had any other verdict been returned."

“Quite so,” replied Holmes, “I must confess I am not familiar with the case Dr. Bell but I fear that we must both face the hazards of the jury making the wrong decision in our work. Our role must be to prove surely and conclusively that what we believe has happened is in fact the truth. Would you not agree?” Dr. Bell concurred and pressed upon Holmes to relate the case of which Watson had been recounting to them prior to Holmes arrival,

“Your colleague,” said Dr. Bell, “gave us an account of the facts as he has recorded them but I am sure that there must be more to it than this?”

“Not at all, Dr. Bell, you will find that my colleague keeps excellent records of my cases. Although at present I can sense a greater interest from Watson on his own activities today than in any detection which I could prevail upon him. May I enquire as to how your day has been my friend?” Watson was indeed feeling exhilarated by what he had seen today and was in turn keen to relay to Holmes news of his day touring the facilities in Edinburgh,

“I must confess Holmes that the work being done in Edinburgh is far more exciting than I had been led to believe. With the like of Dr. Bell and Patrick and their colleagues this must surely be one of the leading seats of learning for medicine in the world.” Bell laughed again, showing his well known easy sense of humour which made him even more personable for that fact,

“John you flatter us, however you say we are only one of the leading seats of learning? Tut Tut, surely we should boast about being the leading seat of learning! Is it not that fact that has led you to consider the position offered by Patrick?” Watson’s face flushed slightly and he looked embarrassed,

“Well, I did say I would think about it, but I have not made my decision as yet.” He glanced towards Holmes who was eating his food with a measured expression which gave nothing away to Watson as to his thoughts on the unexpected announcement. “Holmes, I trust that this does not put us in an awkward situation? I had intended to make you aware of the proposition this evening but I am afraid the cat has jumped out of the sack a little earlier than I had envisioned.”
“My dear Watson, nothing could be further from my mind. In fact you will recall that I did in fact make mention of it this morning that we may well see you in a theatre before the day was out and I believe my intuition was not far wrong. It would be a difficult proposition to resist and I myself would be inclined to give it great consideration were I in your shoes.” Watson felt somewhat relieved by this but could not help wonder if in fact his desertion to Edinburgh would leave such little mark on his friend.
“Thank-you, yes it is an intriguing possibility. I would be sorry to leave you to your own devices again old man, but it may be that you have managed adequately without my assistance today?” Holmes smiled perhaps somewhat sarcastically,
“Indeed Watson, I did manage quite adequately, thank-you. In fact it has been a most interesting day and I must admit I am now very much looking forward to the remainder of my week if today is anything on which to judge.”
“Your meeting with the two visitors this morning went well?” Watson enquired.
“It did, Mrs. Turner proved to be most agreeable and the young constable, Morthouse, well he is young and needs to build up his experience but he is a pleasant enough fellow. I

took the opportunity to call at their house this afternoon to conduct some preliminary investigation into their, situation, as they seem to call it. It was most enlightening, Watson, on several levels." Watson's curiosity was piqued and despite the opportunity on the table he regretted that he had not been a part of the activity this afternoon. It is a funny thing, he thought, how the well intended actions of another can bring about such turmoil in one's mind.

"Were you able to make any progress on their haunting?" asked Patrick.

"I was, very much so, although I think we shall have the matter wrapped up in no time at all. The testimony I received and the evidence laying about the house was enough to tell me the story, but I shall keep that to myself until I can put the next part of my investigation into place. I took the chance to set things in motion which I hope may bear some fruit tonight." Dr. Bell, who had been sitting quietly listening to this exchange turned to face Holmes directly,

"But what of the body, Mr Holmes, that of the lodger Mr Woodbridge? It may interest you to know that I carried out the post mortem on the unfortunate soul this afternoon. Were you able to determine anything in respect of him?"

"Most assuredly, Dr. Bell," replied Holmes, "enough to give me pause for thought on the whole affair."

"I trust you found his spectacles in his room?" Dr. Bell asked, his eyebrow raised, but Holmes did not miss a beat,

"Of course, they were on the night table next to his bed. Which throws up its own questions – why would a man so short sighted try to leave his room without first putting on his spectacles?"

“Quite so,” Dr. Bell retorted, “it would surely be the normal action in such a case to first put these on before going to carry out some investigation.” Sensing that he had missed something Watson interjected,
“I’m sorry but how did you know he wore glasses?” It was Holmes who answered,
“Watson, tsk tsk, it would be clearly obvious from the marks either side of his nose, they would be unmistakable.”
“Quite so…” affirmed Bell as Holmes addressed him again,
“Was the wound on the back of his head a significant one?” Bell pondered this for a moment as Watson and Patrick merely glanced towards each other in wonderment at the game of chess which was opening in front of them,
“I would not say significant but it was certainly consistent with the position in which his body was found. He must have taken quite a fall directly backwards onto the stair. I presume the candle was still upturned in the room when you found it?”
“Correct, you noted the wax dripping on his hand then?” Bell nodded to confirm he had,
“It was clearly a sign that his hand had been shaking and extinguished the candle but also tipping wax out onto his hand. You noted the marks on the wallpaper I presume?” Holmes sat back and smiled,
“Quite clearly….”
“Green?”
“Indeed…” Watson sat forward again now,
“Come now gentlemen, for the sake of us mere mortals watching your exchange please permit us some clue. How on earth did you know that there was green wallpaper in the room Dr Bell? You have never visited the location, am I correct?” At this, Holmes and Bell looked towards each other

and an unspoken understanding passed between them – what had started as a casual game was now becoming a co-operative exercise. Bell turned back to Watson,

"You must know, John, that underneath the fingernails of a person there is a great deal to be found and it speaks as loudly as if we had heard the words from the poor soul themselves. There were scrapings of green wallpaper underneath his nails, or at least I should qualify this by saying only on his left hand. This would suggest to me that he was unbalanced and not in full control of his motion at the time and scrabbled at the wall for support. Was there any further evidence of this in the room?" he addressed to Holmes.

"The carpet runner had been displaced in the same spot," he replied, "as well as some evidence of sweating on the wall from his hand." At this they both sat back and looked across the table, as Watson and Patrick stared back.

"From all that you have said," Watson remarked, "it does not seem so likely that this was a result of some spirit which has invaded the Turner's house. Unless he was so stricken with fear that he was overcome with these symptoms and took a stumble down the stairs striking his head so hard that it killed him." He paused then, and looked carefully at them both, "Although there is one other possibility which would induce such effects on a person, is there not?"

"Laudanum" both Holmes and Bell said simultaneously. Patrick looked surprised,

"You found evidence of laudanum in the lodger?" Dr. Bell nodded solemnly,

"It was evident from the post mortem, clear as day, the smell unmistakeable. What say you Mr. Holmes?"

“I concur, there is no mistake. In fact I am hoping that we shall have some further evidence to this effect very shortly. Dr. Bell, I hope you do not think me discourteous but I have taken the liberty of inviting another guest to join us this evening, one whom I feel may provide us with information which will be beneficial to us both.”

“Really, Holmes,” Watson exclaimed, “do you not think it is an imposition on our host to start putting upon him with uninvited guests?”

“Please John, there is no need for concern,” said Dr. Bell, “in fact by the look on Mr. Holmes face I believe it may indeed be of interest.” Watson settled back into his chair and the conversation moved on to lighter things for a time however the flow was interrupted at around eight thirty by the loud chime of the doorbell which caused a hiatus in the conversation with Holmes excusing himself, with Dr. Bells blessing, to check if the caller was who was expected. A moment later he returned to the room followed by a young man,

“Gentlemen, I have the pleasure to introduce my young friend, Constable Morthouse.” Morthouse smiled and all shook his hand warmly, “Now, constable, if we might offer you some refreshment and you can grace us with your findings this afternoon. I presume that you followed my instructions to the letter?”

“That I did Mr Holmes,” replied Morthouse, “I must admit I was a little confused at first when those street urchins gave me the letter but when I realised it was from you I acted on it immediately. I felt that this was the least that I owed you after your harsh treatment by that idiot Fowler.” Holmes gave a sharp laugh,

“Hah, my good man, think nothing of it, believe me I have come across worse and despatched them accordingly. I believe that you are also on the end of similar treatment, am I correct?”
“He is certainly a challenge to work under, Mr Holmes, that’s all I will say about it.” Holmes took his seat and gestured politely around at the others asking them to retake their seats at the table and they duly obliged, “Now my good fellow, I have filled in Dr. Bell and the good doctors on the situation thus far and now I trust you will bring us some further news?” Morthouse looked a little uneasy, his inexperience again making it difficult when faced with four such learned and reputable persons but he could feel their relaxed state emanating into the room which helped to ease his nerve somewhat.
“Well, Mr. Holmes, after the note had been delivered I did as you asked and made my way to the servants quarters and began to speak to them in general terms on any subject I could pull from the air. The weather I find is always a good topic on which to build a discussion, especially in Edinburgh, followed closely by the latest on the haunting. None of them seemed to me to fit your prediction.”
“What prediction was this, Holmes?” Watson interjected, “You never mentioned you had made a prediction?” Holmes gestured a finger to his lips,
“All in good time Watson. Now go on…”
“Well,” continued Morthouse, “it was when I reached the cook who was busy in the kitchen that I made the discovery I believe you intended. I was chatting to her about some mundane topics when she stopped and gave an almighty sneeze, almost knocked a pot from the stove, such was the

ferocity." Holmes was leaning forward on the table now, his fingertips pressed together, his eyes closed, listening with his usual intensity. "I enquired after her health showing concern for her ailment and she was most ill at ease with it, 'Mr. Morthouse,' said she, 'I've had this terrible cold gone two weeks now and nothing seems up to the job of moving it.' Of course I enquired if she had been taking any remedy for it and she showed me a bottle of cough syrup that she had been taking but in her words it 'was as good as a medicine as I am a surgeon.'" The analogy brought a smile from Patrick and Dr. Bell,

"Did she tell you what she had been taking?" enquired Holmes.

"She did, sir, she had been taking laudanum but her cold had returned with greater impact over the preceding days that she did not feel it was worth her while to spend any more money on the concoction." Holmes stood and walked to the fire, lost in a moments thought and forgetting that his Persian slipper was not hanging on the mantle of this fireplace, turning he said,

"Constable Morthouse, what did you deduce from the information that the cook gave you?" Morthouse shrugged,

"I assumed that the medicine she was taking was perhaps mismatched to her ailment."

"Perhaps…?" asked Holmes.

"Yes, or perhaps that what she took to be in the bottle was not in fact as she expected." Holmes clapped his hands,

"Excellent! We will make a fine policeman of you yet, exactly as I was theorising when I gave you the note. Now, we must try to avail ourselves of this medicine in order to…" As Holmes spoke Morthouse reached into his pocket and

produced a small bottle which he placed on the table, "this is the medicine she was taking, Mr Holmes. I wondered if it may be of help to bring it with me." Holmes just laughed happily while Watson picked up the bottle and gave it a sniff, "It smells like laudanum," he said, handing the bottle to Patrick who concurred, "But you believe that the laudanum has been switched with another substance?" Holmes nodded,
"I do, Watson. If I were in Baker Street now I would be able to analyse this with some simple chemical method to confirm it, but my suspicion is as you suggest."
"Come with me," Dr. Bell said as he rose from his chair, "I have a small laboratory in place in my study, I use it for carrying out simple experiments and analysis and it has what we require to carry out such an investigation of the liquid." They all decanted from the dining room and followed him through the house into a compact room, the walls lined with books and along one side was a table on which were laid out varying chemicals and accoutrements, with more of the same on shelves on the wall above, "Please Mr. Holmes, treat this as your own." Holmes busied himself about the table as Dr. Bell assisted with differing tests on the substance from the bottle. Watson and Patrick looked on, the similarity between the two gentleman not lost on either of them albeit they approached the same crime from opposing ends. After thirty minutes of clinking of bottles and some satisfied murmurs, Holmes and Bell stood back from the table, appearing satisfied with their conclusions.
"Well?" asked Watson.
"What we have in this bottle, John," replied Dr. Bell, "is a clumsily mixed potion of Molasses, Lemon juice and Cloves."

"Cloves?" Patrick said thoughtfully, "I assume added because of their medicinal smell?"
"Quite correct," Holmes exclaimed, "which leads us only to one conclusion. The laudanum which was contained in this bottle was removed and replaced by this mixture. It is an easy subterfuge to carry out on an unsuspecting person who has no reason to suspect any foul play. Why would the cook suspect that anything had happened with her medicine? No, she would quite justly assume that her cold had worsened beyond the reach of the medicinal properties of the laudanum. It seems clear to me that the laudanum which was removed was then given to Mr. Woodbridge in an attempt to put him into a state of confusion and suggestibility. The effects of which caused him to stumble from his room in a drug infused state when he heard the supposed haunting noises, and he collapsed down the stairs, the blow to his head killing him. Which then leads us to conclude only one thing," he paused, striking a match to light his pipe, "that despite the perpetrators original intent, what we are now investigating is a murder."

The evening drew to a close soon after and all bade a good evening to Dr. Bell with their sincere thanks for a most enjoyable evening. The night was cold but clear and in the street were gentlemen returning from their clubs and some of the more unfortunate souls begging for change. As was common at this hour there seemed to be a dearth of cabs available and on their hailing all that was forthcoming was a two wheeler,

“Watson,” said Holmes, “I suggest that you and Doctor Watson take this cab back to Charlotte Square. I believe you will have another busy day tomorrow and I do not wish to delay your return while we wait for a four wheeler.” Watson was about to protest but Holmes cut him off, “I have a small matter to discuss with my new young colleague here and I shall follow on in due course.” Watson nodded but could not help feeling the words from Holmes smart a little, again the feeling of being pushed to the sidelines was apparent. So it was that they left in the cab and returned to Patrick’s home where all but one of the servants had retired for the night. Watson bade Patrick a good night before retiring to his room, slipping eventually into a fitful sleep.

Chapter 11

Watson awoke early the next morning and immediately found his mind contemplating the prospect of waking up in Edinburgh on a permanent basis. The noise from the street outside was noticeably less than one would wake up to in Baker Street which was not an unpleasant experience. There were many opportunities here of which he could avail himself and while in London he may be able to return to his days of general practice, would this be sufficient to sustain his interest? The opportunity to act as a teacher and mentor to the upcoming generation of medical practitioners was indeed a strong lure which was not to be dismissed lightly. He washed and dressed, his mind turning the prospect over during the process, and made his way downstairs fully expecting to be the only one of the house who had risen at this time however this was not to be the case. On entering the lounge he was greeted by the familiar sight of Holmes sitting in a chair, his pipe gently smoking away and a calm look upon his face. "Well, well Holmes, it should not have surprised me to find you up at this hour. Your errand went well last night I trust?"

"All I can say at the moment, Watson, is that it went to plan, the answer to whether it went well should be known to me this morning. You slept well I hope?"

"I slept soundly enough but with so much on my mind it woke me early this morning. The opportunity which has been presented to me here has given me somewhat of a dilemma. I know that you do not need my assistance in your work but I must also consider the matter of our rooms in Baker Street. We were drawn together in the first instance to share the burden of cost on the rooms and I should not like to leave you in the lurch."

"Not at all, Watson," Holmes interjected, "The rooms shall take care of themselves, I am sure I shall find someone to take up the vacant room, although it may take several tenants before I find one who shall put up with my habits quite so admirably as you have." Watson smiled and was about to speak but Holmes held up his hand, and shook his head, "As for your help in my work, you belittle your involvement Watson and I can assure you that your assistance is invaluable. Yet what you must consider utmost in your mind is to choose what route will bring you satisfaction. There is many a man who will choose what others believe is best for him before he will choose what he himself knows is the right decision" Watson sat down heavily,

"That is precisely my problem, Holmes, at the moment I do not know my own heart in the matter. Patrick has offered that I may accompany him again today and….." he paused, "that is to say, Holmes, if you will forgive my desertion of you for a second day? I believe I have a lot to consider." Holmes smiled,

"A three stethoscope problem, Watson." He smiled easily, "No, not at all Watson, please do not concern yourself with me as I am content to my own amusement and I am sure I will find something with which to occupy myself."

"That is precisely what worries me," replied Watson, "When you are left to your own devices there usually is some anarchy which follows." Holmes raised his eyes in mock surprise,

"Really, Watson, you judge me too harshly," however the wry smile around his lips and the twinkle in his grey eyes showing that even Holmes was not believing his own defence. "I may partake of a walk around the city today and may even pay a visit to some of the sights you were so quick to point out to me on our arrival." Watson gave him a rueful look,

"Yes, I'm sure I can see you doing that, Holmes. I would wonder….." His reply was cut short by the door bell ringing three times in quick succession, and upon this Holmes leapt from his seat and strode briskly to the door of the lounge and looked out. Watson followed but could not see who the visitor was but could hear them clearly – the voice was that of a young woman,

"I must see Mr. Sherlock Holmes," she said frantically, her accent quite strong, "my mistress has sent me to fetch him." Holmes threw the door wide and marched into the hallway,

"Young lady, you are sent by Mrs. Turner I presume?"

"Yes, sir, she has asked me to fetch you and bring you to the house." The girl was clearly out of breath and must have been running at full tilt to bring her to such a state, "there was some more trouble last night sir. Please come." Without hesitation Holmes grabbed his coat and cane from the stand in the hall and gestured to the girl to lead the way,

"Come, we shall hail a cab on the street." He followed her out of the door, his parting words fading into the distance, "Watson, please give my apologies to Patrick for missing him at breakfast. I believe I have urgent business….." Watson watched as the maid closed the front door again before turning to give him a stunned look and then walking off in the direction of the scullery. Watson shook his head - exactly as I feared, he thought, when he is left to his own devices!

A short time later, Holmes found himself for the second time standing outside the home of Mr and Mrs Turner watching the police. Constable Morthouse was standing in his usual position on the front step and inside he could see Detective Fowler barking orders to another deputy and then disappearing into the study with Mr. Turner who seemed to be pressing the detective most urgently, although about which Holmes could not make out. Holmes instructed the maid who had fetched him to discretely advise her mistress that he would attend as soon as it was prudent to do so, in other words upon Fowler's departure from the scene. Sometimes, he knew, discretion was the better part of valour. He took his position in the same location as yesterday when he had set events in motion with the note to Morthouse and waited patiently. It was fully one hour before Fowler was observed leaving the house and a few minutes afterwards, much to Holmes satisfaction, Mr. Turner followed with a sheaf of papers under his arm.

Holmes crossed the street and walked briskly towards the house,

'Good morning Constable Morthouse," Holmes said by way of announcing his arrival, before innocently asking, "may I enquire as to the nature of the activity this morning? The maid who fetched me intimated that there had been some further disturbance?" Morthouse shifted uncomfortably and looked around into the doorway,

"Good morning Mr. Holmes, please come inside, Mrs. Turner is waiting for you." Holmes followed him in,

"You have told her nothing I presume of our little subterfuge last night?"

"No," responded Morthouse, "I have not, if it became known then I fear that my neck would yet again be on Detective Fowler's chopping block."

Mrs. Turner was in her drawing room, a small and cosy room which was furnished with a small table and stool in front of the window overlooking the garden, and a comfortable armchair and footrest around which were several books on the floor. She rose to greet Holmes as they entered, "Mr Holmes, thank-you for coming – has Constable Morthouse given you the details of what has happened?"
"He has not madam, but I may be able to shed some light on the matter if I may. I observe that the household is very much on edge this morning which leads me to conclude that you had another, event, shall we say? This was a particularly violent occurrence during which some items were thrown and broken and I would imagine was particularly distressing." Mrs. Turner was struck with the accuracy of Holmes description,
"Mr. Holmes, if you say that Constable Morthouse has indeed told you nothing of last night then I would ask you to explain to me how you come to know so much?" Holmes looked nonchalant,
"Because, my dear Mrs. Turner," he said abruptly, "the disturbance last night was not the result of some phantasm or restless spirit."
"Indeed," she replied indignantly, "and if not then what was it?"
He glanced casually out of the window, "It was me."
"But…." Mrs Turner stammered, "why…." Holmes turned quickly,

“Because this charade has gone on long enough and I am now tiring of the whole matter. It seems clear to me that these so called hauntings have cast their shadow for too long and must be brought to a head.” Mrs. Turner was aghast at his actions but had clearly regained some of her faculty,
“I am not sure I approve of your methods, Mr. Holmes!” she rebuked him.
“My methods Mrs. Turner are not there for others to approve of or otherwise, they are there in order to produce results. Sometimes it is necessary to bang the sewer pipes in order to make the rats run out.” He stepped out from the small room into the corridor and glanced around. Mrs. Turner followed, as did Morthouse who was currently sensing great relief that his part in the matter had not been mentioned, since it was Holmes explicit instruction that he should leave a window to the rear of the house unlatched to allow him ease of entry. Following the disturbance, he had made some great display of immediately searching the house and then checking all of the doors and windows to ensure they were secure, or in the case of that one particular window, locking it again to avoid any suspicion.
“Now,” Holmes said, more calmly now, “I assume from the attendance this morning of the good detective Fowler that the damage caused was not the only outcome? I would not have expected that the detective would be here for only that?”
“Oh no, Mr. Holmes, we have found out something more.” Mrs. Turner replied somewhat shakily, “When we all met up downstairs to check that everyone was safe and well, we found that Annie, our domestic, was not present. Fearing the worst we rushed to her room, only to find that she was gone.

Her bag was packed with most of her belongings and she was nowhere to be found." Holmes closed his eyes,
"You questioned the rest of the staff if they knew of anything?"
"Of course, but they were all as shocked as we were. Do you think that this means that Annie had some involvement?" Holmes shook his head and opened his eyes again,
"I can not say for certain but it would be of interest to see her room if I may." Mrs. Turner led them through the house to a small room at the top of the house. The room was compact and only populated by a bed and a chest of drawers, next to which a wooden chair lay on the floor,
"Thank-you Mrs. Turner, I will not detain you further at the moment. I would like to take a few moments to search the room and I shall come and speak to you once I am done. Constable Morthouse here will assist me and help me to find my bearings if necessary." Morthouse nodded and watched as Mrs. Turner left and disappeared down the stairway.
"What did your detective friend have to say before he left?" asked Holmes, as he stood in the middle of the room, drinking in his surroundings.
"He is not my friend Mr Holmes, he is my superior and could make my career in the police very difficult." "Hah!" Holmes ejaculated, "I have never cared for the term 'superior', in too many cases the person holding the higher rank does not quite fit the description." Morthouse did not comment on the observation,
"He told me most assuredly that I should report back to him anything which I find." Holmes glanced around and caught his eye and pursed his lips,

"Then we must ensure that you have something to keep him happy. Now, tell me what you see in this room constable?" Morthouse looked around from his position in the doorway and shrugged,
"I can see nothing that would be of any help, Mr. Holmes. It is just a normal room."
"Morthouse, you will find nothing from there, come inside and do not just see, but look. You will only see a portion of the room if you are in one spot, you must look up, down and below. The smallest of details may prove helpful to us but already I see something more obvious which gives us some clue. You will observe the chair, upturned clearly in haste during the residents departure, but the bed has not been slept in so what can we deduce from this?"
"That she made her bed prior to leaving?" Holmes righted the chair and sat down facing Morthouse,
"Would you be so tidy if you were fleeing for your very safety? All clothes have been taken and no personal items remain but she took time to make her bed? Would it not suggest that it was not slept in at all, which seems odd given the late hour of the disturbance."
"Of course, so you would conclude that despite the time it happened, Annie had not yet retired to her bed! So why was that and why did she run?" Holmes was watching but did not reply, allowing Morthouse to feel his way through, "Unless she was waiting for something to happen? Or," he said, suddenly realising the significance, "it was Annie who was the perpetrator of the haunting noises and she has fled fearing that she will be discovered!" Holmes smiled,
"Precisely," said he, "although there is one vital element to which you are not aware. Let us step out into the street and

we shall make our next move." They made their excuses to Mrs. Turner, and a few moments later were standing on the pavement outside the house. Holmes began walking around to the back of the house where he retrieved a metal contraption from a bush in the garden to the rear of the house and held it aloft.

"It looks like a pile of old iron- is it significant?" asked Morthouse.

"Indeed it is my good constable, this you could say is the ghost of Edinburgh." Morthouse looked confused so Holmes continued, "before I embarked on my mission last night I made use of the excellent moon to scour the area outside and I saw this contraption concealed underneath the bushes, carefully hidden but the tread from a shoe pointing in the direction of the bush gave away the fact that someone had been there. It is, in layman's terms, a noise making machine – a crude construction but certainly that of someone skilled with their hands. It is this that has been causing the noises, or at least some of them. While this was wound up and working at this end of the house, I believe someone was also moving around the house indoors breaking the vases and causing the damage, but since the noise seemed to come from all around, no-one could pinpoint exactly where it was coming from and therefore it was assumed no human hand could be behind it." Morthouse looked despondent,

"Annie Shurie, she was the ghost? I am ashamed that I have been duped in such a way."

"You and several others, but that is not important now. I was convinced of my theory that it was one of the servants behind this and in taking over the role of the ghost I believe it will have frightened the wits out of her which is why she fled. But

one thing troubles me now…" he paused, "…after the death or Mr. Woodbridge why did she not panic at such a disastrous outcome and flee at that stage? If you were behind the disturbances and it resulted in the death of a member of the household surely you would take fright."
"Perhaps she did not want to draw attention to herself?" Morthouse offered, "if she had left then it would surely have made her the prime suspect? So she decided to stay and bide her time." Holmes nodded slightly but his face did not echo his gesture,
"That may be possible, and it is something we must discover. However, I fear we may also be crediting the poor child with too much premeditation of her actions. In my experience the lowest of the household servants are rarely to be found perpetrating such elaborate hoaxes on their own."
"I wouldn't know about that Mr. Holmes. But it seems that the only question now is where did she run to?"
"That is what we shall now determine, for the one thing a skilled rat catcher will always do is to ensure that he traces his quarry back to their nest. Following my departure last night I took up a discreet position where I may watch the house and as she left I was on her trail. Come now, we must catch a cab and make our way to Leith."

Chapter 12

The cab ride to Leith took them back along Princes Street and then North towards the port. The docks were bustling as usual and the dust and smell hanging over them was like the worst of London miasmas. Holmes was not one who was given to small talk, even with Watson there came a time when it was remarked by his friend that it was like trying to squeeze blood from a stone. But Holmes had taken a liking to Morthouse and wished for him to do well in his career. It was refreshing to find someone in the police who was open to his methods and who was not immediately threatened by Holmes gifts. Of course there was Lestrade in London but one could not afford him the same compliment as was given to Morthouse, since Lestrade invariably would only seek out Holmes assistance as a last resort. "How long have you been with the police, constable?" Morthouse was looking out of the window and was startled by the question, since Holmes had said nothing for the journey so far, albeit only a period of fifteen minutes,

"Only three months, Mr. Holmes. I was to work in my father's legal practice but things changed there and I decided my future was on a different path."

"I presume the change you refer to being the death of your father?" Morthouse was about to ask how Holmes knew this, but stopped, and nodded,

"You recall my saying that Doctor Watson had carried out the post mortem?" Holmes nodded silently, "Yes, my brother assumed senior position in the business and as much as I love my brother I could not see myself working for him. But more than that I could not see myself sitting behind a desk for the rest of my life, it is not my calling."

"You find yourself wishing to be at the sharp end, so to speak?" Holmes said, "How have you found it so far?"
"It is hard, much harder than I imagined. I knew there would be long hours but there seems to be much to learn. Not in the sense of our duties and of the law, those I can master, but there must be a wisdom that comes with being in the police which will take me a long time to acquire."
"It is true that you can not learn this overnight, but from what you tell me I believe you may be sitting on a veritable gold mine of wisdom which should be thoroughly mined."
"In what way, sir?" asked Morthouse.
"Your father was in the legal business for many years?"
"Yes, and his father and grandfather before him - it has been our family business for generations."
"Then you are in a fortunate position." Morthouse could not see to which Holmes was alluding, which frustrated Holmes slightly, "Let me tell you, constable, that I have spent many years studying and perfecting my craft to allow me to advertise my services as the world's first consulting detective. One must learn the periodic table of elements before you can come up with your own compounds and know the cause and effect of each substance. What I mean is that in the files in your father's office, you will have decades of evidence, testimony and methods by which crimes have been committed and then solved and brought to justice. Yes, the wisdom that you must gain has to be developed but by reading thoroughly through the case files in your family vault you will gain so much that others around you do not have access to - you have the ability to build an almanac of crime which will prove invaluable." Morthouse pondered this for a moment but any further discussion on the subject was cut

short by Holmes, "Halloa! Driver stop here please!" They waited inside the cab and during this moment the penny finally seemed to have dropped,
"But of course, Mr. Holmes, I had not thought of it that way, I just looked upon those as dusty old files to be eventually discarded or burned. If I was to study the crimes contained in these folios then you think it would give me the advantage?"
"Most certainly, you will be better able to anticipate the moves of your adversary if you have studied the activities of their predecessors. Don't forget that crime is very often a family business like your own, albeit it from a different perspective. But how does your brother choose a path on which to defend a case in court if not by studying the decisions and arguments from the past?" Morthouse's mind raced through the possibilities and judging by the number of case files in the store of his brother's offices there was a treasure trove to plunder.
"It will be daunting work, not to mention take me some time, but if this is my journey of a thousand miles then it must commence under one's feet.."
"Indeed, that is the spirit, now…" Holmes paused, his eyes darting towards the doorway of a tenement he had been watching, "Look…." Morthouse's eyes darted to where Holmes was pointing and saw that a figure had stepped onto the street and was looking back and forth along the road. "That is our quarry, Morthouse, I recognise her gait from last night, distinctive as it is. I will follow her and see if I can gain any information from her destination." Holmes started out of the cab but held up a hand as Morthouse made to follow, "You must return to your duties…."

"But, surely I can assist, Mr. Holmes," Morthouse objected, "you do not know the area and there are parts that you would not wish to journey into unawares."
"That maybe so," replied Holmes, as he watched the woman gain a hundred yards on them, "but with respect constable, it would do no good to be accompanied by a policeman in uniform. Even if you were to discard your tunic your face could be recognised. You may best serve our cause by returning to your work and passing on to detective Fowler what you have learned from me, although leaving out the news that it was I who carried out the haunting last night, that he must not know. Now, I must go…" He closed the door of the cab and pulled his collar up around his neck and walked briskly after her. Morthouse watched him go, intrigued by the advice he had been given and by the man who fate had allowed to cross his path. Now, to business…

Chapter 13

From the corner of his eye, Holmes glimpsed the black hansom trundle down the street past him, but he did not acknowledge his young colleague as he drifted past. His focus was entirely trained on the young woman who was walking at a brisk pace along Commercial Street, carrying with her a small bundle under her arm and her shawl pulled up over her face to protect her from the cold wind which blew through the docks. The characters that were to be found in the area were not those who would be welcomed in the respectable New Town but Holmes was not unaccustomed to the type and found them to be of little threat. In London his work took him to many an undesirable location or the most raucous of public houses however in the work which he undertook he would avoid nothing in pursuit of his target. However, as he turned the corner, there was a small nagging doubt at the back of his mind that it would have been of some comfort to know that his friend and colleague Watson were at his side with his service revolver stowed carefully inside his coat.

The woman, whom he now knew to be Annie Shurie, thanks to his visit to the Turner's house that morning, was just over five feet in height and of a slight build. She was clearly someone who had worked hard for her living and was not to outward appearances of any means by which she could support herself which made sense to Holmes. Information could normally be bought from the servants of wealthy homes for a small fee but if Holmes suspicions were correct this particular servant had been going far beyond the telling of some back stairs gossip for whoever was putting money

into her purse. It would need to be a considerable sum as she had now abandoned her job and had put up a barrier to future positions as she would have no good reference to present to potential employers.
She came to a public house by the name of the Ship and Anchor and swung the door open and entered without hesitation. Holmes was only a few seconds behind her and was glad to see that even at this early stage of the day the place was busy. Crew from cargo ships mingled with locals and several women plied their trade around the tables hoping for some business. Holmes made his way through the crowd to the bar and ordered a pint of ale before turning to scan the congregation as he drank. Unable to see the girl he sidled casually along the bar just in time to catch sight of her as she handed her parcel to a man sitting at a table in the corner. The man's face was shrouded by his hat but Holmes could make out a scar running down his cheek onto his neck, his chin was covered in a wiry brown beard. Wounds such as that were common on the faces of the people who populated this type of public house and were of no surprise to Holmes. It was as pointless to say that you were looking for a man with a scarred face in such a place as this, as it would be to say you were looking for a man with a walking cane in the New Town. He watched as the parcel was dropped down under the man's seat and the girl turned to walk away but the man grabbed her arm and pulled her close to him. Holmes was poised to act but the man only snarled some words into her ear before releasing her arm and sending her on her way. The girl looked shaken by whatever she had heard and hurried towards the door. Holmes laid his drink on the bar and turned to follow her again but at that moment a man leapt up from a

table in front of him and turned the table in a fit of rage, sending playing cards and coins into the air. Collision was unavoidable and the man turned towards Holmes, his eyes bulging red and his temper flaring,
"What's your game? I bet you're in on this as well aren't you – you look like you would be a bookmaker out to swindle us poor souls here!" Holmes held his hands up in a placatory gesture,
"My good man, I was only here for a drink and now I wish to leave. My apologies if you feel you have been wronged but it was not by me." He made to walk around but the man sidestepped in front of him,
"Some sort of a clever gentleman are we, sir? Too good to speak to the likes of me are we, sir?" The words were spat out at Holmes who again tried to walk past but his arm was now caught and he spun around,
"My good man," Holmes shouted, "I must warn you that this is not a course of action which will do either of us any good." The man laughed, as did his cohorts nearby,
"Oh, I am mighty afraid, I don't think! Who are you to threaten me, you have no meat on you at all that you would stand up to me." The man drew back his fist and swung it hard towards Holmes head, but Holmes was too sharp and ducked to the right to avoid the blow. Holmes was conscious that he was not only losing the trail of the woman but was drawing far too much attention to himself in the presence of the man whom he had seen take the package.
"I do not have the time or the inclination for this!" It was not often called upon but the pugilistic skills which Holmes possessed could be brought forth at any moment. He admonished the man as he brought a controlled combination

of blows raining down on him, felling him with a final blow to the temple. This sudden display of boxing prowess from the lithe stranger seemed to stun the surrounding regulars and Holmes took the opportunity to push his way to the door and out into the street. A quick glance each way saw no sign of Annie Shurie at which he cursed himself for being sidetracked in this way, his gift for avoiding such incident clearly deserting him for a moment. The door behind him was thrown open but Holmes did not wait to find out by whom, but took off into the road where he was fortunate enough to jump onto a wagon as it rolled past with some barrels and he was removed from the scene. His one piece of good fortune being that the woman had seen none of this having left the bar before it had erupted, so his only move now was to return to her building and await her return.

Morthouse had sat back in the cab and cautiously regarded Sherlock Holmes as he passed by him on the way from Leith. He had instructed the cab driver to take him back to the police office in the hope that he would find Detective Fowler there and could pass on the information he had gleaned, which may deflect some criticism at least for the time being. He gazed out of the window at the passing streets and pondered upon the man whom he had just left. He had seemed to Morthouse to be a cold and calculating man but at the same time there was a great humanity contained within that was also apparent. Morthouse could not escape what he had been told by Holmes and it could not be ignored. What he currently lacked in direct experience could not be altered but there was nothing stopping him from learning from the past and trying to apply this to the future. His father had been a great advocate for diligent study and he had grown up with this guiding principle with books never far from hand. All things considered it would be fair to assume that had his father lived on, Morthouse would have gladly partaken of his exams to enter the family business but it was not to be. He could recall his father even saying that 'It is a foolish man who wastes his life on fretting over what may have been rather than pushing forward with what may still be to come.' Morthouse pushed the thought from his head as there was no time now to start pursuing any studies, his time was sufficiently catered for at present with the matter in hand.

On entering the police office Morthouse took a deep breath and steeled himself against the inevitable abuse that was routinely hurled at any constable walking through the holding area. The screams of outrage and the common smells were rife in this area and it was with great relief that he exited through a doorway into another area of the building, the cacophony behind him gradually fading but still ever present as low background interference. Detective Fowler was in his office with the door open, affording Morthouse a split second view of the man before his presence was noted. Fowler was hunched over his desk, pen in hand scribbling furiously in some form of ledger. He was mumbling to himself as he did so and although the volume was too low to discern any of the words the tone was most certainly one of annoyance. Morthouse gave a soft knock on the door and Fowler's head snapped up,
"What do you want?" he snapped, even before he had registered who it was that was standing there. "Morthouse, I am very busy and I hope for your sake that you have some

news for me and this interruption is not without due merit!" This was shouted not so much as a question but rather a demand. Morthouse entered the room and stood before the desk,
"I have sir, since you departed this morning I have carried out some investigation and I believe I have discovered the source of the hauntings at the Turners." Fowler laid down his pen and sat back, his eyes narrowing,
"I see, and what do you believe you have discovered?"
"Upon inspection of Annie Shurie's room I have deduced that she must have left with some haste, her bed had not been slept in and her personal items have been packed and taken with her. It seems clear to me that after carrying out the so called haunting she fled the house in terror at possibly being discovered. I found some form of noise making contraption outside the house which would appear to belong to her as well." Fowler nodded to acknowledge this,
"Credit where it is due constable, that seems like good work. Now, do we know where this Annie Shurie is now?"
"We do sir, she seems to have lodgings of some sort in a tenement in Leith. I saw her there this morning but was not able to apprehend her."
"Again, credit where it is due constable, although my question to you is, are you sure that you came to these conclusions unaided?" Morthouse could feel his mouth go dry and his heart started thumping faster,
"Of course sir, who else would there be?" Fowler slammed his hand down on the desk making the pen jump fully six inches from the surface as he then stood up sending his chair careering backwards against the wall. He rounded the desk and instinctively Morthouse stepped back a pace to try to

keep some distance between himself and the detective, but Fowler was intent on bringing him to within grabbing distance. Morthouse backed up again and found himself against the wall with Fowler standing directly in front of him no more than a foot from his face,

"Do you think I am a bloody idiot, Morthouse?" he raged, "I had occasion to return to the Turner house this morning shortly after I left and was witness to Mr. Sherlock Holmes being admitted by you! What do you have to say to that?"

"Mr. Holmes was there at the request of Mrs. Turner, I had no option but to let him in," he replied.

"Perhaps so, perhaps so, but are you telling me that it was Mrs. Turner who left a short time after in a cab with Mr. Holmes?" Morthouse could feel his head spin and knew that there was now nothing he could say to extricate himself from this situation. He had been foolish to presume that his interaction with Sherlock Holmes would go unseen, especially given the animosity that Fowler seemed to feel towards both of them. "You realise you have deliberately disobeyed my instruction to deny him entry to the crime scene? On top of that you now appear to be colluding with him in following this domestic from the Turner house who may be a suspect in a murder. I should have your guts for garters, Morthouse!" The ferocity of the man in front of him was having an unnerving effect on Morthouse, which he was sure was the exact purpose of this display. Rather like a gorilla beating its chest, it was obviously a well-worn tactic used to elicit this response in its target. But it was within the midst of that fug that he found one small gossamer thread of clarity.

“Correct sir, but that was exactly my intention. I have used this detective to do some of the work for us and let him lead us to where Annie Shurie is now hiding. I thought that there is no point in having a dog and barking ourselves.” Fowler still glared at him,

“That will be your defence will it?” Morthouse nodded, trying desperately to maintain eye contact and not allow his gaze to drop, “Then so be it.” Fowler took a step back and smoothed down his clothing as Morthouse felt the tension lessen in his body. “You will remove yourself from this investigation constable, I am taking charge from this point forward.”

“But sir, you…” Morthouse started to protest but was cut short by a glare from Fowler.

“As I said constable, I am taking charge.” He picked up his pen and straightened the ledger on the desk in front of him, “I suggest that you resume your usual duties on the beat and stay well away from Mr. Sherlock Holmes if you wish to further your career in the police.” Morthouse hesitated for a brief moment, weighing up if it would be of benefit to protest further but he instinctively and wisely decided against doing so.

Chapter 14

In the Edinburgh medical school, John Watson observed as his cousin delivered a lecture to the packed auditorium. The topic of the day, the application of anaesthetic during surgery, had been largely sidelined as Patrick was intent to continue his pressure on Watson to accept the position here. The students were unusually silent and enthralled as Patrick regaled them with tales of his experiences in the Crimea, but as interesting as they were the stories were already taking on the aspect of being from a history lesson. It had been almost thirty years since the Crimean war had ended which was beyond the lifetime of all of the students now gathered. Sensing this and appreciating the need for a captive audience Patrick turned towards Watson and gestured him to the centre of the dais, "My fellow academics," said Patrick, "we are privileged to be joined today by someone whom I hope you shall all see a great deal more over the period of your studies here." He smiled again and Watson tried to demur but Patrick would not be swayed, "Gentlemen, I urge you to show your appreciation for my cousin and former field surgeon, the eminent Doctor John Watson." The auditorium erupted into polite applause as Watson strolled to centre stage and nodded in appreciation of the gesture. Patrick stepped back, his arm outstretched, "Doctor Watson has been offered the position of Lecturer in Battlefield Medicine Techniques here at the school and the faculty believe he would be a great asset. John, why don't you tell the students of your background?" Watson smiled at the array of faces now regarding him, trying to decide within his own mind if this was a situation with which he would wish to be of regular acquaintance.

"Well, my name is Doctor John Watson and I qualified as a doctor of medicine from the University of London," this remark was met with some good natured joshing which served to break the ice, "Yes, thank-you gentlemen, I am aware that this may not be appreciated while I am in Edinburgh. Upon qualifying I took my training at Netley in the skills necessary for field surgery and from there I was enlisted into the Fifth Northumberland Fusiliers in the position of assistant surgeon. It was the intention that I should join my regiment in India but," he paused for a moment as a memory interrupted his train of thought, "sorry, yes, but it was not to be and as the Second Afghan war had just broken out I was positioned instead to Kandahar, deep inside the country." Watson glanced towards Patrick who did no more than encourage him onward and as he looked back to his audience he could see they were becoming more intrigued by this stranger who had been pushed before them. He continued,
"This was a bloody war, and many of the things I have seen I would wish upon no other man. It is most unfortunate that even though that particular conflict has since abated I do not have hope that it will be the last for which young men such as yourselves may be called to action. The injuries sustained by my comrades from incoming artillery, which would go off around us like thunder, were devastating and we lost many good men to the enemy. Similarly I must say that we gave as good as we were given and took out many of their soldiers, the mechanism by which wars are won gentlemen, and by which the futility of the whole affair is most aptly demonstrated. Many honours and medals were won but I could not rejoice in this fact. Would it be only so that we

could settle our differences in a more amicable arena but that is not the way of the world." He paused, feeling himself becoming too introverted and decided to change tack, "it was shortly after that I was transferred to the Berkshires and took part in the ill fated battle of Maiwand." A murmur went around the room as the battle was well-known and the disastrous outcome was a source of some pain within military circles. The British, despite being the superior force in terms of training and equipment were vastly outnumbered by the passionate and fierce Afghans and the battle was long and bloody. Over nine hundred British soldiers were killed and despite three times that number of the enemy being killed and many more wounded it still resulted in a resounding defeat. The complacency of the forces lined against the native tribes was as much to blame as for any other reason.

"I am sure you all know the story of the battle, such is it writ large in recent history, but suffice to say that again my skills as a field surgeon were sorely tested in many areas and more experience gained. This was however cut short when I was shot in the shoulder by a Jezail bullet, my bone shattered but my life mercilessly saved as the bullet only grazed my subclavian artery. I should have been captured if it had not been for some courageous act by my orderly…." He looked up and tried to lighten the morose tone which he had set in the room, "But that gentlemen is another story. Now, I will finish and return you to the capable hands of Doctor Patrick Watson." The students burst into spontaneous applause again and stood to show their appreciation. Patrick returned to the dais and held Watson by the arm to prevent his immediate departure,

"Thank-you gentlemen, I am sure you will agree that Doctor Watson's recent experience and knowledge would be of great benefit. But I see in your faces that you wonder what relevance this may have to your work if you are in a hospital in Edinburgh or in general practice? John, may I ask you to enlighten them?" Watson was feeling drained from his reminiscence but nodded politely,
"My one piece of advice for you as you study here is to learn and relearn your procedures and ensure you can carry them out without hesitation. Yes, I have learned many techniques in the field that I would share with you, and I can give you the ability to improvise with what you have available but they are to no avail if not carried out with great haste. A patient's life may hang in the balance while you try to recall the best course of action but a well rehearsed and well studied physician will not waste such time and will save more of his patients than the former will. In doing so, my other advice must be to beware of the weakened patient contracting a secondary condition. A subject that is again close to my heart since my contraction of enteric fever following my injury was another close call which may have been avoided." Patrick released his gentle grip on Watson arm and smiled,
"Thank-you Doctor Watson, I believe you have given us an excellent introduction to your experience. I hope that our students will be able to make further use of it in the future." Watson smiled politely and nodded his thanks to Patrick and the students before retreating out of the room and into the corridor outside. If Patrick was wishing to force an answer to his offer then it was futile. As he stood in the corridor, listening to the muted voice of his cousin through the closed door, he was in a turmoil of emotions. The feeling of elation

at taking a first step in front of a class was satisfying but below that was a tinge of anxiety, of remembering too vividly his recent experiences in the war and wondering if he was ready to go back into that world, albeit only in his mind.

Chapter 15

It was some time before Sherlock Holmes cast his eyes again on Annie Shurie since losing track of her at the public house. Dusk was just beginning to show its face as the small figure, wrapped in a cloak against the cold, came walking briskly along the street. From his position on the opposite side Holmes was able to see her some way off and was vigilant to see if any other person was with her, however he was pleased to see that she was alone. Annie Shurie walked into the close, disappearing momentarily from Holmes view as he crossed the street and entered silently after her, his keen ears listening for the closing of a door on a landing above. The monograph he had written on the acoustics of buildings was a recent addition to his collection but like all such papers he had studied the material most thoroughly.

As he rounded the stairs and arrived on the third floor he looked carefully on the floor for any telling sign and as suspected the dust and dirt outside one door had been recently disturbed. Holmes listened carefully but could make out no noise from within so taking his chance that he would not be outnumbered he struck the door firmly three times. There was a brief scuffling noise but no-one came to the door and no voice called out. Holmes pressed close to the door, "Annie Shurie, I know you are in there and I would recommend for your own sake that you open the door." Still nothing, "my name is Sherlock Holmes and I am here on behalf of Mrs Turner, I have no involvement with the police. I only wish to get to the truth of what has happened, but I suspect you may be innocent."

"I am innocent, I've no done anything," a quavering female voice replied.
"Then you have nothing to fear, except for the police and I fear that I may be the only one able to help you. If you please…" He waited patiently until footsteps could be heard and a bolt slid back and the door opened.
Annie Shurie peaked through the gap, her face wrought with worry and her eyes filled with equal parts of fear and suspicion, "What do you want, mister? I've done nothing." Holmes smiled,
"I believe that may exactly be the case. I have been engaged by Mrs. Turner, your employer, to discover the source of the disturbances which have been plaguing their home. I know now that you were that source." She was about to protest but Holmes piercing stare silenced her, "Come now Miss Shurie, let us not waste our time," said he sharply, "we both know that you were behind the noise but what I want to know is why. In short, I may be the only chance you have to prove your innocence to murder."
"Murder, I've nothing to do with that! They can't say I was anything to do with the lodger." Her face was now panic stricken, "You say you can help me?" Holmes nodded, "then you better come in then." Holmes entered without hesitation, closing the door behind him and following Annie in to a sparsely decorated room where she pointed him to a wooden chair and she took up position on a mattress on the floor.
"You are lodging here with someone I presume?" enquired Holmes.
"Yes, my sister, she's out working just now, won't be back until morning most likely."

"You admit, Miss Shurie, that you were behind the noises and the night time episodes?"
She nodded,
"I was, it was only a joke at first, something to do in the night. I had been speaking to a friend of mine and she said I wouldn't be able to do it but I did, even that daft policeman they sent couldn't catch me."
"Your creativity is to be much admired, I'm sure. But, I wonder why you did not make yourself known to the police when Mr. Woodbridge was killed." She looked confused,
"Why do you keep saying he was killed? It was an accident, wasn't it? That's what I was told – it must have been my fault. If I hadn't been doing all the mischief then it wouldn't have happened."
"It is possible, but I have since come across new information, but I must ask you to tell me all that you know about the circumstances that night." She was lost in thought, wringing her hands red,
"I don't know," she said, "he would kill me if he finds out."
"Who, who do you fear Annie? I can assure you that you are quite safe." She laughed, a tremor clearly audible,
"Hah, that's what you say mister. I'm no so sure though, he already told me to keep my mouth shut or I'd be for it. You better leave mister, I can't tell you anything, that's right, I've nothing to say. I don't know anything." She rose from the mattress and stood nervously in front of Holmes, badgering him to get up and leave.
"Why will you not tell me the name of this man? I can help to have him apprehended, he will not be able to hurt you or even find you, the police can ensure your safety."

"Hah, the police! They're worse than he is, now go, get out or I'll scream for help." Holmes stood, wishing to avoid a further scene today and walked towards the door, opening it and then standing in the doorway, preventing her from closing it. He spun around with some speed, taking her by surprise,

"You would be well advised to tell me who you are protecting. If you choose to keep silent then I will have no option but to have you arrested for the premeditated murder of Mr. Arthur Woodbridge, lodger at the Turner house, Heriot Row, Edinburgh."

"But I didn't have…."

"Then do the honourable thing and give me the name of…."

"He told me to tell no-one, I don't think he wanted any harm to come to him, he was very fond….he thought he was like a son……." Holmes relaxed his posture and gave her as warm a smile as he was capable of mustering,

"You mean Mr. Turner, it was he who persuaded you to continuing with the haunting?" She burst into tears, her hands covering her face and dirt streaking down her cheeks,

"He told me he would see me on the streets if I told anyone…." Holmes took a step onto the landing and put on his hat,

"Yet here you are in any event. I shall do my best to explain the situation to Mrs. Turner and request a good reference so you may gain employment. But for now, I urge you to keep your own counsel and do not tell anyone of our meeting." She nodded slowly, still in a state of despair and confusion and closed the door as Holmes walked down the stairs to the street. Mr. Turner shall keep until tomorrow I believe, he thought as he pulled on his gloves, for now, back to my lodging to see how my friend has fared today. He strolled off in the direction of the city centre and as he did so, unknown to the usually alert Holmes, a figure who had been skulking on the landing above, crept down the stairs and stood facing her door.

Chapter 16

On Thursday morning, the ritual that was breakfast was a curious affair in as much to say that there was a palpable atmosphere in the room. That is not to say that there were any unpleasant feelings between the participants but that each was clearly consumed by some preoccupation on their respective minds.

Watson was still in a state of some confusion concerning his reaction the previous day while describing his experience in Afghanistan. It had been some months since his return and yet during the lecture he had what could only be described as an emotional resurgence of the feelings and memories from that period. While Patrick had witnessed this, although his knowledge of the feelings within Watson was limited, his concern was focused mainly on the question of whether his cousin would take up the position for which Patrick had fought to have him offered. Unknown to Watson, it had not been a foregone conclusion for his appointment which had taken no small amount of persuasion from Patrick and now this wobble, as he had perceived it, was a concern. It was Holmes who perhaps was the least troubled by what occupied his mind, but instead he was relishing the case which had come quite out of the blue and was a welcome addition to his sojourn to Edinburgh. Travel may broaden the mind, it is said, but for Holmes travel was generally a means to an end to investigate some case or other.

It was clear to him now that while the supposed haunting had been started as an ill advised prank by a servant it had been used to mask a darker objective. Holmes mulled over the possible reasons why the lodger, Woodbridge, had been the target of this rather amateur murder. It could be clearly seen that the manner in which the crime had been perpetrated was most clumsy. Not only was the evidence of foul play easily detected, by Sherlock Holmes in any case, but to involve a third party in the charade was unforgivable. Holmes knew of many criminals and had respect set aside only for those whose work was carried out to a similar standard to his own, which was few and far between. Holmes train of thought was interrupted as Patrick broke the silence,

"Shall you be accompanying me to the medical school again today John?" he asked.

"Yes, yes I will, it should give me great pleasure. Unless that is, you should wish me to accompany you Holmes? You could perhaps make use of me in this case?" Holmes took a moment to withdraw from his thoughts during which time the Doctors Watson looked slightly uneasily towards each other, neither sure if the question had been heard or was perhaps of no interest.

"I do beg your pardon," replied Holmes, "please do accompany Doctor Watson today, you shall find it far more rewarding than this case I believe."

"Is it not proving to be enough of a challenge for you, old man?" enquired Watson.

"It is singularly uninteresting at the moment," Holmes said, not entirely truthfully, "I believe we are dealing with that worst of criminals."

"Do you mean murderers, Mr Holmes?" offered Patrick.

"No," laughed Watson, "he means amateurs. Honestly Holmes you are too much." Holmes gave a sharp laugh and stood abruptly,

"I shall take that as a compliment, Watson, now if you shall excuse me I shall take my leave." He did not wait for any further response before gliding swiftly from the room, leaving Patrick and Watson to finish their breakfast before leaving to their day's educational pursuits.

Holmes strode off in the direction of the Turner house, breathing deeply as he went to fill his lungs with the fresh morning air. It was indeed a blessing that given Holmes dislike for the countryside that such refreshing air could be found within the city. Contrary to his expectation the weather was mild and this morning there was not a breath of wind, the sounds of the carriages echoing loudly as they trundled along the cobbled street. On turning into Heriot Row, and in sight of his destination, he became suddenly aware of some rapid footsteps behind him. He swung around and was confronted by a red faced and breathless Morthouse, his face stricken with panic,
"You had better come with me, Mr Holmes." The look in Morthouse's eyes put paid to any protest from Holmes, "I have a cab around the corner here." Moments later they were making their way at a gallop to Leith,
"I presume," said Holmes, "that we are going to the abode of Miss Annie Shurie?"
"We are Mr. Holmes, and I must warn you that the matter has become very grave indeed." Morthouse would elaborate no further, insisting that Holmes view the scene for himself to form his own thoughts on the matter. A short time later they were ascending the stairs of the close in Leith and, as they approached the front door, Morthouse stepped aside and gestured Holmes through the door, "I have seen it already,

Mr Holmes, and I should prefer if I did not look on the scene again."

"I would strongly suggest you accompany me, again you must take longer to observe the evidence rather than just look. Clearly I am about to walk in to a room where someone's life has been taken and we owe it to the victim to take the opportunity to see what they are telling us still."

Morthouse nodded reluctantly and followed Holmes along the hall through to the living room. They stopped inside the room, with Morthouse feeling the same revulsion he had experienced earlier but for Holmes his detached, analytical mind was processing what was in front of him. The body of Annie Shurie was strewn like a rag doll over the mattress which was saturated with blood, the dark red liquid seeping onto the floor. She had clearly been beaten and her features were almost unrecognisable from the swelling and bruises which covered her face and shoulders.

"Tell me what you see, Morthouse," said Holmes.

"Well," Morthouse spoke hesitantly, remembering the earlier lesson, "she has been attacked with some force, there appears to be knife wounds across her arms and hands."

"Quite so, Morthouse, but I beg you not to fall into the same trap as many others to observe only the obvious. I could bring in any passing stranger from the street who could tell me the same facts. We must look behind what is obvious." Holmes walked over and kneeled down close to the body and gestured Morthouse to join him, "Look here, the angle at which the blade strikes the body demonstrates a person with a preference for his left hand."

"Then surely that is to our advantage since those people are fewer in number?"

“Correct, and I would venture that the wounds on her arms are from her efforts to defend herself. Now, what was the condition of the door when you arrived?”
“It was closed but not locked, I was able to push it open with little effort. You believe she may have opened the door to her attacker?” Holmes smiled slightly,
“Indeed, you are learning. If this had been a random intruder then the door would be burst open. I also observe that the room is only in a state of minimal disruption, a few items displaced, which tells us that this was not a burglary which has gone awry.” Holmes stood and gazed down at the body,
“The focus of the beating is on the face which from my experience, at least in this circumstance, suggests a very personal vendetta against the victim.” Morthouse stood back up again,
“Then we should look towards her family or friends?”
”I don’t believe so, I am afraid that I do not believe in coincidence and the fact that this has happened so soon after her fleeing from the Turner house will have a connection. This would seem to me to be an attempt, and a successful one at that, to ensure that Annie Shurie did not tell us anything more than she has already.” Morthouse glanced around at Holmes,
“She told you something?” Holmes relayed his discussion with Annie from the previous day. “Then we must arrest Mr. Turner immediately!” Morthouse exclaimed.
“No, not yet. While we have the connection we have no direct link to Mr. Turner. But I do not feel that such a man as he, a banker and one who contains himself within that world, would be capable of such rage and physical violence. But for him to pay a man that would do this would not be out of the

question, he would not stoop to soil his hands on such a task I believe"

"But," said Morthouse, "where would a man like Arthur Turner seek out such a man as would do this?"

"That is what we must discover, there are still pieces to this puzzle to be uncovered," replied Holmes.

Chapter 17

Holmes stepped in to the street and made his way on foot back towards the public house in Leith to where he had followed Annie Shurie the previous day. Morthouse had summoned assistance to deal with the body and the prevailing wisdom was that it would be better if Holmes were not present when they arrived. Holmes could see that there were the makings of a good detective in Morthouse but it would take time to draw him out of his current thinking. He must learn to think outside of his usual manner and learn to question more of what he sees before him.

The Ship and Anchor public house had lost none of its drabness from the previous day and neither had it gained anything which would recommend it. The idea that Mr. Turner would have frequented such a place as this was inconceivable to Holmes. He would have been not only highly conspicuous but would more than likely have been a target for thieves and garrotters. With Holmes having drawn such direct attention to himself already to the regulars of this place, it was now dangerous for him to return as he currently stood. One thing of which he was acutely aware of was that while the regulars of this public house may not be the most learned, they had the memory of an elephant when it came to faces and recalling a wrong done against them. If the man who had tried to assault Holmes was frequenting the bar again then the result would most surely be the same as on the last visit.

Taking this into account and marrying this against the desire to investigate inside the bar the latter won out and therefore a means to achieve this was required. In London, Holmes had at his disposal a wide range of disguises which he could call upon but here in Edinburgh he was without his array of accoutrements however that being so, it was no great disability to one whose creative resourcefulness had been well honed over the years.

Holmes walked further down the street towards the docks and spotted some rough looking fellows waiting near a tramp vessel who regarded him cautiously as he approached, but were decidedly more affable when his pocketbook was produced. After a short period of discussion, hampered by their thick accents from Eastern Europe and rapid discussion amongst themselves, a deal was struck for the supply of one overcoat, one hat and a small bag which was strung over one of the crews shoulders, all in return for fifteen shillings which would undoubtedly be frittered away very quickly on drink or on the women who frequented the port looking for business.

Donning this new attire over the top of his own and smearing some dust around his face and over his boots and trousers, Holmes affected a slight stagger as he returned in the direction of the Ship and Anchor. Inside, the bar was again crowded and the air thick with tobacco smoke, noise and opinion. A few heads glanced casually around and looked at the man entering but no-one took any particular note since the new addition to their circle was clearly one of their own. In a dockside bar such as this a stranger's face was nothing extraordinary. Holmes made his way to the bar and ordered a pint of ale which he drank deeply, there being no place here for slow sipping of a drink since the pace was hard and quick. Finding a chair unoccupied in one corner he sat down and sat with his head back against the wall, giving the appearance of a man in a drunken sleep but his eyes were open by the smallest fraction to afford him a view of the room. There did not seem to be a minute go past where some shouts were not heard and the potential for a brawl erupted between two or more drinkers. This was common and of no real concern for Holmes as in most cases the men would square up to each other before backing down on request of a friend, their respective pride saved for the time being. Holmes sat patiently for over one hour, every so often taking a small drink before falling back asleep, and as was hoped, a man then entered which made Holmes take note, the scar on the mans face as prominent as ever.

As before the scarred man took a seat at a table which was situated on the opposite side of the bar from Holmes. There was a large enough crowd that prevented either man having a clear look at the other but as Holmes was of no significant interest to anyone, being taken for another drunk, he was able to watch his target through the bustle of bodies without suspicion. The previous time Holmes had sighted the man it had been only for a brief moment since events had quickly overtaken him and he had been forced to leave. However, afforded the luxury of time by his disguise, he was now able to make a closer observation. The man was around five foot ten inches in height and his clothes were old but were held in good condition, not the type of attire one would expect from a common worker or resident of the poorhouse. This man was clearly of some means but perhaps was keen to portray to the average person a façade of being one of the poorer inhabitants of the city. As he lifted a pint of ale to his mouth, Holmes could see on the inside of his arm a tattoo which he could clearly identify as the marking of one who had been in the merchant navy and was a branding familiar to Holmes from his study of these forms of body art. The man did not appear to be acquainted with anyone else in the bar, however his eyes were continually scanning the room as if looking for a particular person. After fifteen minutes of this, and Holmes maintaining his careful watch, the door to the public house opened and through the crowded room another man approached, carrying a small box, no bigger than one foot along each side and wrapped in brown paper. The knot was unclear from this distance so nothing could be gleaned and due to the infernal movement of people across his field of vision, and this new addition having his collar turned up and hat pulled down, Holmes was not able to see his face. The man sat down with his back to Holmes and leaned in close to the scarred man, whose hands could be glimpsed sliding a small notebook across the table and words were exchanged. Although the man had his back to Holmes, through his careful observation, he could see the posture of the man tense and his shoulders tighten as he sat back in the chair, shaking his head. The scarred man leaned in more intently now, his mouth close to his acquaintances ear and Holmes opened his eyes more now to try to see better what was being discussed. The throng of people moving to and fro in between them was an unfortunate distraction, giving Holmes a view of the two men as if viewed through a zoetrope where the picture was there but the detail in between each frame was omitted. Holmes keen vision was trained in on the scarred man's mouth trying to discern the words being said but through the visual interruptions he could only make out some brief phrases which made no clear sense – time to act, decision taken, orders from, three more boxes – and most chillingly of all – no witness to remain. Holmes cursed his position and wished he could be close enough to hear what was being exchanged between the two, and was contemplating how this could be achieved when the scarred man sat back again, eyeing his cohort with a piercing stare and smiling coldly. His opposite number at the table seemed to make some return remark judging by his gesticulations but then nodded and rose to leave, the box he had brought with him being slid discretely along the floor with his foot towards the scarred man.

Holmes cursed the lack of his faithful Watson at this stage as there were now two suspects which required to be followed. In times such as this Watson would gladly follow one while Holmes maintained a trail on the other but this time it was not to be, a decision must be made on which to follow. On the one hand the scarred man seemed the most likely candidate but at the same time he was identifiable and a man with such prominent marking as he displayed would most likely be known to the police. But this other man was a new component in the equation and was not identified as yet, a matter which in this case Holmes elected was the greater need. The scarred man and the contents of the box could be brought to light in good time but it may yet throw light on the whole affair if the identity of this other man could be gained. It was in such moments that decisions must be made and it was part of the success of Holmes in his chosen trade that he was accomplished in choosing the correct option.

In anticipation of the stranger leaving, Holmes rose from his chair and, affecting the same staggering walk, he made his way through the bar and out into the street where he quickly crossed the road and waited for his target to emerge. A few moments later the familiar sight of the hat and coat which had been seen inside came out of the door and with a final pull of the brim over his face the man walked, head down, in the direction of the city centre. Holmes walked parallel to the man on the other side of the street, his stagger now discarded to throw any familiarity from his gait that may show him as being the man who had left the Ship and Anchor. It was seldom that such details were noticed by the common man but in Holmes profession it was prudent to assume that the person with whom you were dealing was more of the uncommon kind, particularly when some scheme appeared to be in play. They had gone only a few hundred yards when the man hailed a passing cab and as the carriage was stopped for the man to embark, Holmes quickly ran to the rear and slipped himself onto the luggage shelf in a move practiced previously but not without its hazards.

The cab travelled from Leith, through the centre of town and onwards to yet another area with which Holmes was not familiar. The old town of Edinburgh was the counterpoint to the wealth and prosperity inherent in the New Town. The closes here were narrow and tenements rose high above on each side, with poverty, disease and crime rife throughout the area. The cab stopped on the High Street and Holmes jumped down from the rear and walked casually away as the stranger disembarked and paid his fare. Holmes turned and followed as the man walked someway up the hill in the direction of the Castle before turning in to a close, as Holmes did likewise to keep a track of his quarry. A few paces later the man turned into a tenement building with Holmes trailing him up the stairs, finally hearing a key slide in to a lock and turn with the door opening and closing shortly after.

Having taken note of the address and deducing that it would be of no further benefit to maintain a watch on this person at the moment, the detective decided that a return to town and with luck a meeting with Constable Morthouse for an update may be beneficial.

Chapter 18

The scene of Annie Shurie's murder had been yet another unfortunate occasion when the paths of Constable Morthouse and Detective Fowler had crossed. Morthouse was in the process of overseeing the body being removed from the flat when Fowler arrived sooner than had been expected. His face was fixed with his usual dark glower when he came through the door of the flat and in to the main living room,
"What's the story here Morthouse?" Morthouse was growing tired of being barked at in the abrupt manner which Fowler frequently emitted but responded dutifully,
"Murder sir, Annie Shurie, one of the maids from the Turner household. She has been stabbed and beaten quite viciously sir."
"What do you make of it? Have there been any clues found?"
"Nothing of note, sir." Fowler cast him a withering glance,
"I think I will be the judge of that constable, unless that is you have been recently promoted to detective?" Morthouse could feel his defences rise,
"All I have determined is that the murderer was left handed and it would seem to be an attack by someone who knows her, we have no sign of entry being forced in to the flat. Nothing more is known."
"There were no witnesses then I presume?"
"None," replied Morthouse. Fowler watched him carefully, and Morthouse wondered if his earlier visit with Sherlock Holmes had in fact been witnessed. However Fowler proceeded to have a look around the room,
"Alright then, since you have nothing more to tell me then I suggest you secure the rooms and be about your duties."

"Yes, sir." Morthouse replied, as Fowler took himself outside, with Morthouse watching after him curiously. Is this how the detectives of our force conduct an investigation into a murder scene? It is of no wonder then that Mr. Holmes has such low regard for them and I am inclined to see his position. It led Morthouse to think back again on Holmes advice to him; that study of previous crimes was as good an education as could be gained in this profession if not from first hand experience. The body having been removed, and Morthouse's role at the scene completed the thought to return to his regular duty on the beat was not in the least appealing. Having been removed from the case at the Turner house, he could not bear to return to the mundane reality of his current posting therefore perhaps some other form of policing could be employed.

Morthouse found himself a short time later climbing the stairs to the office of Morthouse and Morthouse and to his satisfaction there was no noise from the rooms above. He had known that there was a good chance of his brother being away on court business this afternoon and was pleased to take the opportunity to have unfettered access to the files and documents which were stored in their father's old office. Despite ongoing cases at the time of his fathers' death, sufficient time had elapsed by the time his brother had taken up the reins that matters in these cases had moved on and the services of Morthouse and Morthouse were no longer desired. It was unfortunate to the name of the company that they had been unable to complete these cases but under the circumstances it was perhaps understandable, and far be it from Morthouse to cast any aspersion on his brother.

Morthouse opened the door to the office and stood in the doorway looking inside, trying at once to both remember his father in place in his office and also to block out the painful image of the last time he was seen there. The memory is a fickle device however and will not allow one image to be seen without also producing those that one did not wish to see. The office of his father was largely untouched apart from some tidying of files into a pile on the corner of the desk, his brother having decided to remain working at his own station rather than immediately move to his father's desk. Not quite the same as avoiding walking in dead men's shoes but largely the same principle. Morthouse looked at the cabinets where the case histories were kept and pondered the best place to begin his research. In conclusion he decided, as with all jobs, the best road in was to start at the back and work forward. Although this would require him to carry the many files from the cabinets to the desk, such a method would give him the cases where the information was most complete. It also saved him the job of trying to make sense of what was lying on either end of the desk which was in some disarray. While perhaps not the reasoning which would be acceptable to the meticulous Mr. Holmes, it was certainly more than acceptable for Morthouse. Starting at the lowest drawer in one of the cabinets, Morthouse was surprised to find the files in a state of some disorder, an unusual occurrence given his father's particular tendency towards meticulous order. My brother must not share this trait, he thought, cursing him for no doubt putting the files in any space available rather than in their rightful order. However, the files passed across the desk in front of him with rapid succession from one pile to join another, with occasional trips back to the cabinet for more, but the cases being mostly of little note; petty thefts and robberies which, while low in value, would still result in the perpetrator being given a lengthy sentence or transportation to the colonies in some cases. As he went through more of the files, the disparity in the laws, or in particular the justice meted out was evident. Those with the least in society were treated with no allowance for their circumstances, but then as a constable of the police he knew that there was no alternative but to level the full force of the law when it was required. It was tedious work and in reality the information which was available in the first dozen files was for the most part of no particular interest. The most informative being a thief who had carried out a deception on a jeweller and had made off with a large amount of pearls and jewellery to the value of three hundred pounds after posing as a European count. Morthouse skimmed the next file, already thanking his good fortune that he had decided against the career which was waiting for him in the law. However, as with most means of employment the day to day grind of the mundane was the bread and butter with the exceptional only coming along once in a blue moon. The names on the documents almost blurred as he read quickly through and put the file aside on to the read pile, but then he stopped. It was almost as if his subconscious had registered something that he had not noted and it had taken a few moments to connect. He grabbed the file and opened it again in front of him, reading through the notes:

Accusation of theft of large sum of money from Edinburgh bank, removed without authority from victims accounts.

Bank threatened to foreclose on his business if he did not keep up the extra payment.

Victim Mr. Charles Lamont made claim of intimidation and threats to his life in return for payment of cash to protect his business.

Regularly visited by group of men recognised from Old Town and of thuggish appearance demanding further payment.

The notes continued in this regard for half a page and what was clear was that this man was being extorted for protection money and if he did not settle then his business would be closed down. Although this was not uncommon in this day and age, it was the last two lines which particularly caught Morthouse attention:

Victim has laid accusation at the door of Mr. Arthur Turner, owner of bank, as being behind said extortion.

Addendum: Case closed, no further case can be brought at this time due to accidental death of Mr. Lamont before trial. No other witnesses to testify.

Then scrawled underneath, again in his fathers hand;

Cross reference with Hastings and MacDonald cases…

Morthouse scrabbled through the files remaining on the desk, casting them aside on the floor until he found the two mentioned. Quickly looking through these he scanned down

the comments which again gave brief details of the current status of the cases. Both were closed due to the disappearance of the key witness prior to the trial. Morthouse sat back, the three files open on the desk in front of him and took in what he had read. Are these telling me that the people involved in these cases have been removed or murdered? Could Arthur Turner be behind such acts? Morthouse was no expert but the thought that Turner, a prominent person in the Edinburgh community would be capable of carrying out such outlandish schemes seemed highly incongruous. Fraud and extortion possibly but murder?
Morthouse quickly closed the files and hurried out of the office and down the stairs with only one thought in his mind. Sherlock Holmes must see these.

Chapter 19

John Watson stood over a cadaver in the anatomy theatre and surveyed the elevated rows of students watching intently for him to begin. The room was a vital part of the school's training but from his perspective in the middle he could not help feeling it was also slightly gladiatorial. He was the one in the ring with the crowd all leaning over the row in front trying to afford themselves of a better view of the blood and gore being revealed below. He did not know the identity of the body on the table but the sight of a corpse covered in a white linen sheet was already making his mind race. He could not fathom his reaction to this since he had seen death many times during his campaigns with the army and it was not unknown during his time with Holmes. Perhaps it was the necessity on this occasion not to try to heal but to deconstruct this body, this person, on the table in front of him. He had seen too many comrades struck down with him the only hope between life and this state of death now before him. Perhaps the memories of those instances are still too fresh in my memory to be buried in the past, he considered.

It was a rumble of impatience that drew him from his thoughts and he glanced around before drawing the sheet slowly back to reveal a pallid body and a face calmly asleep the way it had never been in life. Watson glanced at the poor unfortunates face and to the wounds inflicted on his torso, "As you can see gentlemen, this man has been stabbed several times by a small blade causing blood loss sufficient to render the man unconscious leading to death." The students watched on, waiting for further analysis but Watson had drifted off in to his own analysis, "We must wonder what brought him to this point," he said, "to lay upon the table here before us to be drawn and examined. Yes, we shall be grateful to him for the knowledge that he shall impart to us now that he is no more, but we would not have cast our eyes in his direction during life." Watson looked around the auditorium, catching the eye of many of those watching, some of whom seemed intrigued but many only keen for the dissection that followed. "This man, gentlemen, is now a mere textbook. Not only can we learn anatomy from him and to identify the organs and structure of his corpse but if we were to so choose we could learn of his life and his habits…." He trailed off, his thoughts turning to those whom he knew could read such information which was beyond his skill. He wondered at the location of his friend Holmes and what events were transpiring in the investigation being carried out at this very moment. It was to be conceded, and Watson was well aware of the fact, that in front of him at this very moment he was involved in an investigation of a different kind but the turmoil within him was not conducive to the task in hand. He stood back, clasping his hands at his side and turned to Patrick, "I am afraid I feel a little unwell Doctor Watson, I should be grateful if you could take over this lesson." He did not wait for Patrick to interrupt with any question or objection but simply handed the surgical implements to him, "Gentlemen, if you will excuse me." With that he gave Patrick a stilted smile and a nod and then walked past him to leave the auditorium and leaving the building into the street outside intent on putting some distance between him and the medical school to allow the fug in his head to clear.

Sherlock Holmes paid the cabbie for his fare from the High Street back to Patrick's house and then entered to discover that he was the only one there, aside from the servants. Taking this as an opportunity to mull over the pieces of the case he sat himself down in a chair in the lounge and took out his pipe, filling and lighting it and drawing the warm smoke in and exhaling it slowly. The case in hand had been an interesting diversion when first arriving in Edinburgh and he was glad of at least some small stimulation to make his travel worthwhile, however as the week had progressed further details had been revealed to show that this was a more complex problem than had initially been foreseen. Who was the man bearing the scar in the Ship and Anchor public house and what was the mysterious package of which he had taken delivery? Who was his presumed accomplice whom Holmes had trailed back to the Old Town and what was his part in the scheme? There were questions yet to be answered and Holmes would be reluctant to leave Edinburgh on Friday without coming to a resolution on this case, even though it was not up to the high bar set by some of his previous investigations. However regardless of this fact it was not within his nature to leave a matter unsolved. Holmes had been in the chair for some small amount of time when the silence was interrupted yet again by the bell ringing at the front door. A few moments later the familiar voice of Constable Morthouse drifted through the house enquiring of the whereabouts of Mr. Holmes.

"I am in the lounge, Constable Morthouse," Holmes yelled without leaving his chair, "pray come through and bring me up to date with your situation." Morthouse appeared in the doorway, out of breath and red faced,

“Mr. Holmes, I beg your pardon sir, I have some information which I believe may be key to our case.” Holmes smiled at the use of the word ‘our’ however in truth he must concede that it was always beneficial to have an assistant, and as his Boswell had abandoned him then he must adapt accordingly. ”I see you have been in some rush to come here. Can I presume the information you have is of the kind that will move us forward in the matter?” Morthouse nodded,
“Indeed,” he sat down in a chair opposite Holmes and opened up the files on the small table between them, pointing out the relevant notes to Holmes whose interest was again piqued. “As you can see Mr Holmes, in each case my father has pointed the finger towards Mr. Turner.” Holmes nimble fingers deftly flicked through the pages of each file,
“It is becoming very clear, Constable Morthouse,” he exclaimed, “that we are dealing with the most pernicious of crimes, that of extortion. From these files the suspicion is that Mr. Turner has been using his connections at the bank to extort money from these victims. I must use the word victim advisedly since there seem to be more sinister forces involved if these men were despatched or removed before they could give their evidence to the court.” He read over one of the files again, his machine like mind sifting through information trying to place one of the names he noted there, however it seemed to lurk in the shadows just out of his reach.
“These are just the files which I found in my father’s office,” Morthouse offered, “given time there may be more to uncover.” Holmes rose from his chair, scooping up the files in to his hand but stopped suddenly catching Morthouse’s attention as the cogs in his head locked on to the name he had been seeking. Turning on his heel he kneeled on the floor at

the side of the chair and rifled feverishly through the newspapers which had been left there as fodder for the fire. He stood up and turned to Morthouse, holding up a paper in front of him, open to the fifth page and, rustling it violently as he did so he thrust it out in to Morthouse's hands,

"Hah! I knew that the name in the file was known to me, please cast your eyes down the column Morthouse."

Morthouse scanned down the story which told of the tragic events which had occurred in the gas explosion a few weeks earlier, the name of the deceased striking him like a slap across the jaw,

"My goodness, Mr. Charles Lamont! He is the accuser of Turner who died supposedly in an accident, by this account a gas explosion. Do you feel that this has a more sinister explanation Mr Holmes?"

"I am certainly of that mind and I believe the very person that can cast further light on the matter is Turner himself. What I have in my hand," said he, waving the files in front of him, "should give us enough leverage to question Mr. Turner further and if we can put him under sufficient pressure then I do not believe him to be strong enough to withstand. His earlier bravery whilst I was in his house was very much bolstered with the presence of Detective Fowler so we must ensure to question Mr. Turner now on his own."

Let me fetch my coat while you go outside and hail us a cab." Morthouse ran out of the front door while Holmes adorned his coat and picked up his cane and followed. In the short time that Holmes had taken to carry out these tasks and follow Morthouse outside, the familiar figure of John Watson was standing talking to the constable, both standing next to a four wheeler.

PART 3

Further excerpts from the journal of Doctor John Watson

Chapter 20

On leaving the medical school, my mind in a rage of confusion, I took the decision to partake of a walk and return to Patrick's house in the hope that this would serve to clear my mind. It being mid-afternoon the streets were busy with people, carts and carriages trundling along the streets, goods and people being carried through the city. My love for Edinburgh was blurred by my feelings towards the job offered to me here, yet I could see many positives to Edinburgh life but something would not allow me to commit. I could feel the lure of London calling to me and there was my friendship with Holmes also to consider. I walked at a brisk pace, trying to exhaust some of the nervous energy which was racing through my body. My nights rest had been poor, lying awake for many hours pondering which course to take, but still I seemed overcome with confusion. I had resolved within my own mind to make my decision by Friday since we would return to London on the evening train that day, if that was my will, and I should also like to give Patrick my answer sooner rather than later.

As I approached Patrick's house, my attention was caught by the door opening and the young constable whom I had last seen at Doctor Bell's raced out and hailed a passing cab. He spoke with the driver and then opened the door but did not enter. "Good afternoon constable," said I, "you seem to be in quite a hurry, is there some development?" He turned to see who it was addressing him,

“Doctor Watson, yes, we have some new information that Mr. Holmes wishes to act upon, it may be a good lead in our case.”
“That sounds like good news, may I ask what the lead may be?” He stalled slightly and I could sense a reluctance to tell me, perhaps to avoid saying something which he should not. I was about to push him further when I heard the door bang shut to my left and then a familiar voice shouted down the path to greet me,
“Watson!” said Sherlock Holmes, “you have been released from your duties early today I see. Have you no better pursuit to be about than loitering here in the street?” He fixed me with a wry smile, his grey eyes twinkling despite themselves.
“Good to see you also Holmes,” I replied, “Constable Morthouse tells me there is some development in your investigation? May I accompany you and perhaps you may bring me up to speed?” Holmes gestured towards the cab with his cane,
“But of course, Watson, it would be my pleasure. We should move swiftly now as time is of the essence,” said he, leaping up the two steps in to the hansom, closely followed by Morthouse and then myself. Holmes tapped sharply at the roof with his cane and we moved off in to the Edinburgh streets.

“So,” Holmes asked, “can I ask how things are faring with Doctor Watson and the medical school?”
“Very well, Holmes, very well indeed thank-you.” I knew this to be an untruth but for some reason I could not bring myself to admit defeat at this stage, nor to elaborate in front of Morthouse. There seemed little to be gained at this point in

trying to explain what I did not fully comprehend myself, there would be time enough for that once I had made my decision. "Now, pray tell me of the latest on your case?" Holmes explained to me the progress which had been made thus far and, handed me three files which I examined closely and I could see that matters were very likely about to be brought to a swift conclusion.

"So you believe that Mr. Turner is using his position to blackmail these poor people? Why would he do such a thing? Surely in his position as an executive with his bank he has means enough that he would not stoop to such low behaviour?" Holmes laughed haughtily,

"Hah, you know as well as I Watson that such men are often tempted to live beyond their means and will go to any length to sustain the illusion. Let us not allow ourselves to believe that such practices as may be commonplace in London are not also in evidence in Edinburgh. However, we shall speak to Mr. Turner and see what he is willing to tell us. Halloa driver, stop here!" Holmes rattled the roof of the carriage again with his cane, drawing us to a sudden stop, "I wish to arrive on foot and not alert anyone to our visit by pulling up in a carriage with the incumbent noise of the horses. Come…" he opened the door and swiftly stepped out and started marching up the street with Morthouse and I in pursuit. Holmes was a contradiction at times, swaying from states of such morose despair that I would hardly expect him to leave his rooms again to the state which he now displayed – the ecstasy which came from the thrill of the chase, his preferred drug of choice.

Our knock on the door was answered by a maid, "Good morning," said Holmes, "we are here to see the master of the house, is he available?"
"I'm afraid I shall need to check, sir," she replied, "if you would be so kind as to wait here." The door closed again and her footsteps could be heard diminishing along the hall.
"She might have allowed us to wait inside," I said.
"I would suggest that she has been instructed to allow no-one to enter without approval, given the circumstances there may be reporters wishing to try to gain entry for an easy exclusive." We waited only a few moments and when the door opened again we were faced with Mrs. Turner,
"Why Mr. Holmes, Constable Morthouse and, I am afraid I have misplaced your name, sir?" I reminded her of our brief meeting previously, "yes of course, do excuse me. Please come in all." The door was pushed wide and we stood in the hall but a second later. "I understand you wish to see my husband?"
"Indeed madam, on a most pressing matter," Holmes intimated to her, "would you be so kind as to show us to him?" She smiled graciously but a little coldly,
"But of course, just as soon as I check if he is at liberty to receive you. He would seem to be very popular today, you are the second visitor in a matter of minutes."
"And the first was…?" Holmes asked.
"Oh, no-one of note, just a lad with a package to deliver to Arthur." She walked a little way down the hall to a door and raised her hand to knock.

The explosion which came at that moment rocked the house to its foundation and the door of the study splintered on its hinges, sending debris flying in to the hall. Mrs. Turner instinctively shielded her face but the force of the blast knocked her from her feet and she crumpled to the floor. As is often the case with such moments, the scene seemed to play out every detail more slowly for our eyes to capture. From within the study, a bright flash of light flared and then disappeared just as quickly to be followed by smoke drifting out of the doorway in a grey plume advancing towards us. I could see before me Morthouse's face wracked with shock as he stood motionless, paralysed by the almighty thunder clap which had accompanied the explosion. Holmes was already moving forward, his handkerchief held over his mouth to try to prevent choking on the smoke. I found myself rooted to the spot for a moment, my mind again spinning furiously, the memory of such noise and chaos being only too familiar to me from the campaigns. Whether through design or simply my military training taking control of my actions, I hurled myself forward and threw myself down to the floor to tend to Mrs. Turner. Her dress was torn and blood was flowing on her arms and legs, her screams and cries cutting through the house bringing the staff running,

"Get back," I shouted at them, "it may not be safe, get out of the building by the back door and stay clear!" They also seemed in a state of paralysis at the scene before them and I roared at them again to which they finally responded. I quickly examined Mrs. Turner further to determine the extent of her injuries however was thankful to find that they were superficial in nature. No broken bones were apparent but she was in a severe state of shock. I followed her gaze from the hallway in to the study and saw Holmes crouching over a body whom I presumed to be Mr. Turner.

“Watson!” yelled Holmes. I ran into the room but could see straight away that the case was lost. The force of the blast had decimated the room, with the remains of a sturdy writing desk splintered and scattered around the floor. Beside this was the body of Arthur Turner,
“It’s no good Holmes, there is nothing can be done for him now.” Holmes stood back and surveyed the room while I found a dressing gown on a nearby chair and placed it over the body. The sight of her husband with his arms removed to the elbows and severe damage to his chest and face was not something which Mrs. Turner should have to deal with at this moment. Later there would be no choice but for now she must be shielded as best we could mange. I walked back to the hall and noticed that the servants had filtered back along, their curiosity too much to let them stay outside. We guided Mrs Turner into the lounge and sat her down and I asked one of the maids to stay with her and give her a brandy, while I returned to the study.
“What do you make of it Holmes? Can I assume that this is not what you were expecting to find here?” Holmes was standing in the centre of the room, his sharp eyes flitting from one spot to another, taking in everything that he could gather from his surroundings.
“Indeed Watson, in fact this has moved things to another level entirely. I had thought that Turner would be our culprit but this would now seem to me to be someone trying to clear up a trail which may lead to their door.”
“You think that someone was using Turner?”
“That I could not truthfully say, though Turner would not appear to be the lynchpin in the matter he was certainly a cog in the machine. Look here, amongst the debris lying around

the floor." I took a close look around my feet, the mahogany of the desk was specked with some other lighter wood.
"What is that Holmes?" Holmes picked up two pieces of the lighter wood and handed them to me,
"Look carefully Watson, this is a different wood, and look, the residue upon the pieces." I ran my finger over the wood, the surface disrupted by the heat from the explosion.
"Shellac?" I offered.
"Correct," Holmes replied.
I was familiar with Shellac, a resin which is secreted by the female Lac bug and when processed is used as a varnish for wood, not only for its appearance but also as a good defence to seal out moisture. "Very elaborate, do you believe that this was what contained the explosive material? Why go to so much trouble when the box will be destroyed?"
"Quite simple Watson, if you must send an anonymous package to a man like Turner then you must be sure he will open it. Some common piece of wood or a carelessly wrapped parcel may be set aside or opened by a servant but if the item looks to be of value then you can be sure, or at least as much as one can be, that the recipient will believe it to be of some interest. I find it unfortunate that the contents of Mr. Turners desk have been obliterated by the explosion, I fear that we will have lost some vital evidence." I was struck by Holmes lack of compassion towards the dead man still in the room with us,
"Holmes, have you no sense of feeling about this man's death? He lies here not three feet from us and you are lamenting the loss of evidence!" Holmes sneered towards the body,

"Watson, I shall save my mourning for the true victims in this case and not those who die at the hands of those who are participants in the whole affair. I am afraid to say that Mr. Turner was as guilty in this matter as whoever sent this infernal device."

"What do you mean Mr Holmes?" I looked around and saw Mrs. Turner standing in the doorway, her eyes red and she was clearly in a state of considerable distress, "How dare you say such things about my husband." I could see Holmes was still in his analytical frame of mind and from his expression as he turned I could see he was about to assault her with logic and reason which would not be helpful.

"Mrs. Turner," said I calmly, "I believe I told you to stay in the drawing room, now please." I tried to guide her from the room but she would not budge, her gaze fixed on Holmes, as much I believe to demand an answer from him as well as to keep from looking at the gown stretched out on the floor covering the body. I gave Holmes a glance which he thankfully recognised and his posture softened slightly, removing the edge which he was known to employ at times.

"Mrs. Turner," he said, "I am sorry to tell you this but your husband was involved in a most hideous crime. It is my firm belief that he was not only extorting money from people who had invested their money and trust with his bank," he paused briefly, "but also that he killed your lodger, Mr. Woodbridge." Mrs Turner staggered against the door jamb,

"He can't, he wouldn't do such a thing," she tailed off, her body shaking, still in shock and trying to comprehend what was before her now.

"I do not say these things to simply add to your distress Mrs Turner," said Holmes, "but I am almost certain that your husband gave your lodger a high dose of laudanum which caused him to hallucinate and fall down the stairs. Whether murder was his intent I cannot say but that was certainly the result as surely as I stand here before you. Furthermore I am confident that your husband has been murdered here to ensure his silence. By whom I do not know but I assure you that I will find out, if for no more reason than I believe the lives of others to be in danger also."

"How do you know this?" I asked.

"Because I have seen the men who are responsible, although at that time I did not know what their game was to be. I followed a man from a public house in Leith to a tenement in the Old Town. He had delivered a small box to a man in this public house and three more were requested. We can safely assume that this was one of these boxes therefore we have three more which I am sure must be destined for the same purpose." He gave one final glance around but finding nothing of particular interest he made to leave but stopped by Mrs. Turner, catching her gaze with his piercing stare, "You saw the person who delivered the box?" She said nothing for a moment, still stunned by the revelations,

"I…I did," she replied, "he was only a boy of perhaps ten or eleven years old. I took him to be a messenger sent by the bank, I did not question him on the delivery."

"Quite so, and neither would you be expected to, he was a perfect cover." I followed Holmes out of the room with Morthouse trailing behind as we exited the house,

"Do you think we should find this boy Holmes? He may be able to tell us some vital clue?"

"I do not believe we have time, in any case he is not material to this matter. If our culprit is capable of carrying out such an atrocity he would be careful not to reveal his identity. Pursuing the lad may only endanger his life also. No, we must make our way to the High Street and find out what we can from the man I followed." Both Morthouse and I made to follow Holmes along the street but Holmes held up a hand,

"Morthouse, this is a police matter here, I suggest that you remain and deal with your colleagues and arrange to remove Mr. Turner to the mortuary. I suspect that there may be an imminent visit from Detective Fowler so I urge you to bring him up to date with what we now know. Doctor Watson and I will pursue this other lead." I sensed that Morthouse wished to protest at being left from the pursuit of the next suspect however being an officer of the law at a crime scene I believe he could see that he had no option but to remain and therefore reluctantly deferred accordingly. "Watson," asked Holmes, "I presume you are not carrying your service revolver?" I nodded,

"I did not think I would have any need of it at the medical school," said I.

"Then we shall make a quick stop by the house to collect it. I fear that we may not go through the day without being glad of its presence."

Chapter 21

I had to admit to myself at this point that being back on the trail with Holmes was bringing me immense satisfaction. I had come to Edinburgh to enjoy a relaxing break with my friend, and also to get to know my extended family a little better than I had previously, however something was preventing me from enjoying the holiday as I would have expected. When I gave thought to the previous few days as we journeyed back to Patrick's house I could finally see that what I had been feeling most was almost a sense of resentment for the way the trip had evolved. From leaving London with a positive attitude I had come to Edinburgh and was faced with asking myself searching questions which I was not yet ready to answer. Some may say that within the human mind all such questions must be answered and there is no opportunity to hide from them but there are ways to suppress them. Once done then they can be locked in to a small part of your mind without need to give them consideration or daylight until one was ready and engaged to do so, and for me that time was not now. I should be grateful to Patrick for offering me the opportunity which was presented to me here and I know he had nothing but my best interests at heart. But in doing so I believe he had pushed me in completely the opposite direction from that which he wished. My injury sustained in Afghanistan was almost completely healed physically, but mentally, I now knew that those scars ran deeper and would take the longest to mend.
Holmes and I disembarked from the cab and went in to the house where I ran up the stairs to fetch my revolver from the case in my bedroom, while Holmes went to the kitchen to

fetch some supplies since we would inevitably miss supper that evening. As I returned downstairs, Patrick was waiting for me in the entrance hall,
"John, are you well?" he asked of me, "you left suddenly from the school that I was concerned but I had to attend to the students." I nodded and placed a hand on his arm, "I am fine Patrick, let me assure you." I had intended to speak with Patrick tomorrow but in the current circumstance I felt that there would be no more appropriate time than the present. I guided Patrick towards the drawing room and explained to Holmes on his return from the kitchen that I would be no more than a few moments. His impatience was clearly visible to me even though I believe he was trying to disguise it but in any event I must set matters straight with Patrick.

Patrick threw a log on to the fire and it roared back to life in the hearth as he stood facing me, his hands clasped behind his back, "Do I presume correctly that you have made your decision John?" I nodded, but could not as yet bring the words forth from my lips. Was there still some indecision in a corner of my mind? I had been through every eventuality on my walk back from the medical school earlier but now that it came to the point of no return I could feel the hesitation within me again. I continued regardless,
"I have Patrick. You must understand that the offer which has been made to me here is most generous and I am entirely in your debt for such an arrangement. But I am afraid I must decline your offer of the position here." Patrick did his best to disguise any feeling he had toward this but I saw the involuntary but fleeting lowering of his eyes and the subtle

movement in his face which gave away his disappointment, my acquaintance with Holmes making me somewhat sharper at picking out these discreet signs.

"You must follow the path you feel is right for you John. May I ask if anything here has swayed your decision in returning to London?"

"The opportunity here has been a difficult one to refuse," I replied, "but I believe that to spend every day immersing myself in the methods of battlefield medicine would do me no good. I must focus on moving forward beyond my experiences in the war and this would only serve to make me dwell on it even further."

"I had a feeling that something was on your mind, I would be blind not to see it, and yet I hoped that you would feel differently. So you shall remain in your current situation with Mr. Holmes in London?"

"Indeed, that is where my interest lies at present. It is a pity that during the course of the week you have not been able to take the time to know him better, he is an intriguing fellow. But no matter, my work with Holmes both as his biographer if you will and his friend and colleague keep me well occupied at the moment. In time I would not be at all surprised if there is a book to be published on my times spent with Holmes in his investigations. You would scarcely believe some of the matters upon which his expertise is requested." Patrick smiled and walked forward and shook my hand, his other hand pressing the back of mine,

"Let this not be a passing meeting though John. You are family and you are welcome here any time as I hope you know? I should be very sad if this turned out to be the first and last opportunity we had to get to know each other. But I speak of this too soon, we still have tomorrow before you depart." I became acutely aware at that moment of movement outside the door,

"We do, Patrick. Now I am afraid you must excuse me as Holmes and I have some business which must be attended to." I turned on my heel and opened the door to reveal Holmes standing waiting for me, his impatience still on display, "Now Holmes, are you ready?" He was already walking to the front door and held it open,

"I am Watson, and you?" I walked forward and stood in the door, surveying the street outside as I put on my hat,

"I am."

Chapter 22

The evening was drawing in as we walked up the High Street, the noise and bustle again evident here, as everywhere in the city, but in this area it was not a pleasant or relaxing noise. Gone were the noises of people about their business, at least any business one would wish to be involved in if one was a gentleman, and gone was the sight of couples and families taking the air. Replacing it was the smell and noise of the lower classes who were frequenting the public houses and who lived in the tenements leading off the main thoroughfare. Patrick had relayed some of the story to me earlier in the week during one of our quieter periods and it was in knowing how the city had evolved that I came to understand the city more clearly.

The New Town where Patrick and many others lived was, compared to the rest of the city, a recently constructed area having been completed during the early part of the century. The result of a competition for architects and designers to give Edinburgh a new horizon, the New Town was the grand plan to move the gentry and wealthy inhabitants to a new suburb. The medieval streets and tenements of the Old Town were crammed to the gunwales with people and there was no room to grow there, due to the streets clinging to the side of the hill leading to the volcano on which the castle was built. These streets had once offered protection within the city walls when there was risk of attack but now they were home to tanners and butchers working on the street and all manner of people living cheek by jowl in the many closes. It was hardly surprising that in such close confinement and in this poverty that the living was hard, disease a daily hazard and crime was seen as a way of life. In the brief period of time since we arrived on the scene this evening there were groups of men idling outside the bars, haranguing passers by and starting fights but the police seemed powerless to intervene. I found it both inexcusable but at the same time perfectly explainable given the circumstances within which the people lived in this area.

Holmes led me up the hill and stopped outside a close on the right hand side of the street. The noise emanating from within was difficult enough to bear from this distance that I did not know how anyone could live in such a place. I chided myself for thinking such a thought and reminded myself that I lived in a style of some privilege in London and should not forget that this was not the case for most people in any of the cities of the Empire.

"This is the place, Watson" said Holmes, "I followed the man here yesterday whom I had seen speaking with the scarred man at the public house in Leith. He must live within that tenement just there," he pointed to the first door just off the street, "but the question is how we shall proceed."

"I say we should go in there and find out where he is and take him to the police, surely?" Holmes shook his head, his eyes fixed on the doorway,

"But what would that gain us Watson, aside from one easy collar? We must remember that there is a greater threat here and the man we are seeking may yet have three other packages to deliver. There are possibly many more lives at stake." We moved over to the side of the street and found a dark corner where we could stand and look as if we were discussing some business or other matter. I stood with my back to the close and Holmes kept watch, scanning the street for the man we sought. “I could not help but overhear your discussion with your cousin earlier, do you feel you have made the right decision in returning to London?”

“Nothing will get past you Holmes, will it? Even a private and confidential conversation?” He gave me a flicker of a smile and I laughed,

“If you will speak of such matters when there is a detective in the area it is unavoidable my dear Watson.”

“Yes, so I see, and to answer your question, I do believe I have made the right decision. The work at the school is impressive and I should like to hope that one day I can make a contribution. But for now, I am not ready to up sticks and move to the other end of the country when I am only just finding my feet back in civilian life. I feel I have a foundation in London on which to build a new life and I am not ready to cast that aside. Anyway, Holmes, someone must keep a record of your activities, wouldn’t you agree?”

“Pah!” said he with his usual mocking tone, “your obsession with writing these down will come back to haunt us I am sure. Now….”

He pressed a finger to his lips and then deftly swerved around me as I stood, leaving me wrong footed as I made after him.

“Is it our man Holmes?”

“Yes,” he yelled over his shoulder, “and empty handed at that.” I could see the figure of a man disappearing in to the close opposite but we were in there after him,

“I thought you wished to wait until you knew if he had delivered the packages? I whispered.

“That would be an ideal scenario, however since he is without any package at the moment then we can only hope he has them still in his lodgings but, in the worst case, he may

have delivered them already. Speed is of the essence, we must determine the fact of the matter and then act upon it accordingly." Holmes darted in to the close and up the stairs at speed, his energy far outreaching mine. By the time I arrived on the second landing he was standing outside one of the doors, his ear pressed against the wood and his eyes closed.
"What do you hear Holmes?" I whispered. He merely shook his head and his brow creased at the interruption. He listened for a few seconds longer before gesturing to me to remove my service revolver,
"Be ready now, we must be quick and decisive before anything can be done by our suspect." Stepping back a pace Holmes aimed a kick square at the door which broke open and we fled in to the lodging. Once inside, the rooms were small and bursting with clutter. A makeshift desk was set up along one wall of the sitting room on which was a partially made box, surrounded by tools of the carpenter's trade, some rags and small shaped pieces of wood which appeared to my eyes to be remnants from the construction. Holmes had already turned upon the occupant of the rooms and as I did likewise I was greeted by a sight which I was not expecting. My impression on entering was that we should be on the trail of a murderous and evil villain who must be stopped on all accounts. The bomb which had exploded at the Turner house had shaken me to my core, my nerves now squarely on edge and my heart pounding furiously. Since working with Holmes I had become accustomed to such feelings but this one was amplified many times. Not since the battle in Afghanistan where I had been injured had I felt such a combination of fear, anger and determination. But as I turned

and raised my revolver at our supposed enemy I was immediately struck that one's impressions based on expectation are often found to be wide of the target. The man was not standing defiantly before us, his weapon of choice aimed in our direction, but was cowering in the corner of the room, his hands held up to shield his face,

"Please, do not shoot," he yelled, his panic evident, "I have the box ready for you." I cast a quick glance towards Holmes who was observing the man keenly but his posture had relaxed slightly,

"Holmes," said I, "what do you make of it?" He did not look at me but merely raised a hand to gesture for me to lower my revolver which I duly obeyed. The man in the corner of the room did not lower his hands but I could see through his fingers the terror in his eyes was quite genuine. "You say you have the box ready?" Holmes asked sharply, "why has it been delayed?"

"There was not sufficient time, sir, your master did not give me sufficient time. He wishes me to provide him with works of craftsmanship but it is not possible in the time he allowed to me. The boxes I have provided this evening already, were they in order?" It was plain to see the man was in a state of great fear and I wondered if Holmes' game of following this poor unfortunate's lead was the best method to employ, however it seemed that Holmes had concluded his game,

"I am sure they were exceptional my good sir, if they are to be judged alongside this current work on your table here." The man's countenance started to change to one of confusion, "But….you are not here to collect the final box?" he lowered his hands now and I saw a youngish man, perhaps no more that twenty two or three years of age but he was thin and

clearly in want of a good meal. Holmes had turned away and sat on the small stool in front of the table and was examining the box,
"You are a craftsman sir, I must commend you on your work, the joints here are most skilfully done." The man said nothing, I believe trying to fathom out who were these two strange gentlemen who had barged in to his lodgings. "Look here Watson," I allowed my gaze to go over towards Holmes, "dovetail joints hold the box together and also on the small drawers here. You can always tell the work of a craftsman Watson, not only by the finished article but even by examining the sawn edges. A novice will find the sawing action clumsy and will disrupt the surface of the wood, making it rough, but here we have smoothly sawn, neat edges," he paused for a moment, "interesting indeed," he said as he turned around on the stool and leaned forward to face the man. "My name is Mr. Sherlock Holmes, a detective investigating this case, and this is my colleague Doctor Watson, may we have the pleasure of your name my good man?"
"It's William Joyce sir," he said, rising now from his crouching position and walking towards us and sitting on a small bed, "but why are you here if not to do with my….." he seemed to search for the correct word, but Holmes helped him,
"Business? Would that be a fair description Mr Joyce? Now, if I am not mistaken you had an order for three such boxes, where are the other two?"
"Gone sir, delivered. I was behind with my work but I was summoned with the two boxes I had ready since they were urgently needed."

“Summoned by whom?” I asked.
“I can not say sir, they….” He looked like he would break down but pulled himself together, “….they have threatened my family, that is my wife and child and I do not wish to chance crossing them as they are clearly men of their word, as ill as it may be.” Holmes nodded and sat back,
“Do you know the purpose for the boxes you create here?” Joyce held his head in his hands,
“What would you have me do, condemn my own family to death? I have no choice but to make these infernal devices and then I shall be released from my obligation to them.”
“Hah,” said Holmes startling the man, “I am afraid you are much mistaken if you believe they will simply allow you to walk away from your part in this vicious business. I believe that you do not even know the half of it but I will say this to you, my colleague and I witnessed earlier the intention for your device. We saw a man killed before our eyes on opening the package delivered to him with his family left without a husband or father.” I could see the thought having its effect on the man despite Holmes white lie concerning the Turners having a family, and I am sure they would not be left short of money regardless of the circumstances.
“But why are you laying this at my door, sir? I may have made these devices but I did not deliver it to this man you speak of, nor did I have any intention to kill anyone. My only concern is to finish with these people and to allow my family to be able to live free from the threat which hangs over us all now.” His face was wretched with anguish at the thought of this but I knew Holmes must persist with this course,
“Your family will not be safe,” said Holmes directly, “in fact I believe it may be more truthful to say that neither you nor

your family will ever be able to sleep soundly. The man who was killed today, a banker by profession, we strongly believe to have been a part of the scheme which has been taking place here, but his part in fact was as one of the key conspirators in a game that was bringing great rewards." There was a slight glimmer of realisation which I noticed on his expression but the penny had not quite dropped the full way as yet. Holmes continued,

"Do you believe that if these men are capable of murdering one of their own that they will stop short of eliminating you also? You, who is able to not only identify them but to lay bare the methods behind their blackmail of you and their use of your, devices, as you call them?" The man stood up and wrung his hands furiously,

"Then I must escape, but then how can I go when my family will be murdered in my place? I am caught squarely in a trap from which I am unable to escape!" The extreme agitation before me was unbearable to watch,

"Holmes," said I, "we must do something here surely?" Holmes closed his eyes slowly, his face as calm as a mill pond but his mind clearly calculating furiously behind,

"The only way Mr. Joyce can remove himself from his predicament is to assist us to find the men responsible and we shall have them put behind bars. Once that has been achieved then you and your family shall be able to carry on your lives, although I would suggest a change of location. A man with your skill as a carpenter will not have any trouble finding work, I am sure, in perhaps Glasgow or some other city where some measure of anonymity will be assured." Joyce sat down again on the bed,

“Then I have no choice but to put myself in your hands Mr Holmes.”
“Quite so, I am afraid. May I suggest in the first instance you give us a very quick recounting of all you know of your employers and on your clever device here?”

Chapter 23

It was only some twenty minutes later that the three of us were in a cab, headed towards Leith. I sat next to Holmes and opposite to us sat William Joyce carefully holding a small, but very deadly, wooden box on his knee. Both Holmes and I listened with growing interest as Joyce recounted his tale while completing the box we now saw before us. I had been privileged during this week to watch some skilful hands at work during my time at the medical school but this man's hands were their equal. He fitted the components together with speed but at all times with a sureness of touch and eye for precision that was a clear sign of a master of his craft. I had to remind myself several times that this was not a craft in which to be in awe but of which to be fearful under the circumstances. In saying this I could only feel pity for the predicament in which Joyce found himself,

"I was approached by a man in my small workshop," said he to Holmes and I, "he chatted to me for some time and asked to see some samples of my work and I thought no more of it Mr Holmes. But the very next week as I was returning home from my work I was grabbed from behind and bundled in to a carriage, the next thing I knew I was in some lodgings being instructed to build this contraption. I did not wish any part of it but I was told quite clearly that should I refuse then it would be to the detriment of my family. I asked them exactly what this meant and was told in no uncertain terms that my wife and child would be taken from me. Well, Mr. Holmes, Mr. Watson, I ask you, what was I to do?"

"Indeed," said Holmes, "can you describe the men who man-handled you and brought you to the lodging?" He had shaken his head,
"There were none so remarkable that I could recall them Mr. Holmes, there are so many similar men around this part of town it would be impossible to be sure. The only man that I can describe to you in such detail would be the one who seemed by all appearances to be in charge of the gang. A man with such a vicious tongue in his head and I could honestly say gentlemen that he would seem to be of a mind to take great pleasure in the pain inflicted on others. It was for this man that I have not gone to the police or taken my chance to escape. It was this man whom I met yesterday in the public house in Leith where we are now headed. He instructed me that he would need three more boxes further to the one I delivered to him. I tried to protest, to tell him that I had fulfilled my side of our bargain but he became angry, told me that I had fulfilled my side when he told me that it was so."
"Yes, I saw your exchange yesterday as I was on the opposite end of the bar disguised as a sleeping drunk. I followed you back to the lodgings taking you to be in league with the man although there was something amiss in the exchange. What is the name of this man?"
"He never gave me his name, he said I will never need to ask for him as he shall either seek me out or shall be where he says he will when we have to meet."
"Then we shall not keep him waiting any longer."

So it was with this said that we had departed the tenement and caught the cab in which we were now travelling. There was one piece of information which was still eluding me

however, “May I enquire exactly how these devices work?” I asked, directed towards Joyce but it was Holmes who answered,
“My dear Watson, I should have thought a man of your experience would have deduced that from watching the construction?”
“I could see there was the outer casing and within three small drawers which appear to act as one when either of the handles are pulled, but as to the mechanism to cause the explosion I could not quite see.” Holmes sniffed,
“I can see it will be to your benefit Watson that you are returning with me to London, still much to learn I fancy. Mr Joyce, if you would be so kind?” Joyce nodded,
“Well Mr. Watson, the principal is a simple one – it is just like lighting your pipe. We have a match, or in this case a wad of matches drawn together in a bundle, and we have material to offer the combustion and explosion when the drawer is opened.” I was still baffled,
“But how do you set light to the material?”
“This is the part in which I would take some pride had this been for innocent uses but I am afraid my own craftsmanship has acted against me since I have created what I believe to be one of its kind. Behind this drawer here,” he pointed to the front, “there are small pins which are attached to strings. These in turn are connected to small pieces of match paper and at each side the cluster of matches are fixed, so that when the drawer is opened, it will pull the paper along the matches and set them alight. The flame is conducted by means of a small pipe from the chamber in front to a separate chamber behind where the gunpowder is tightly packed, along with a sizeable amount of gun cotton. As you have seen from your

description of the explosion this afternoon it is quite effective and the materials contained will give off quite a reaction." I sat looking at the box on his knee, to all intents and purposes no more than a decorative set of drawers as you would keep cuff links or sewing materials in but within was a design of such brilliance due its very simplicity and effectiveness.
"Incredible," said I, "so when Mr. Turner pulled open the drawer after opening the package earlier today, he unwittingly set off the device and caused the explosion which killed him."
We rode in silence for the next ten minutes until Holmes requested the cabbie to stop and we alighted in to the street several hundred yards from the Ship and Anchor public house. Holmes set Joyce on his way instructing him to deliver the box as was required and then to retire from the premises and go back to his family whom he should remove to a safe hiding place. Joyce concurred with the plan and gave us the details of a cousin he knew where he believed they would be safe and would wait for word.

Holmes and I took up position across the street and watched as Joyce entered carrying the box. It was now dark and the hour getting late in the evening with the area surrounding the bar and down towards the docks not a place for the faint of heart. Crew from the vessels in port mingled with prostitutes in the docks and all staggered from one public house to another, their constitutions surely being tested to the extreme.
"It is hard to believe," I said, "that this is the same city where we have spent the last few days with Patrick. It feels as if the New Town area is a rose in between two thorns."

"All cities have their dark and their light Watson, as we have seen in London, although I must confess that this area in particular does not make me rest easy."
"What do you make of the story which Joyce has told us, do you believe him?"
"I do Watson, he seems to be most genuine and his fear and panic were as real as I have seen. We can only hope that we can give the man some peace of mind before the night is out.....wait now, he has come out again..." We watched as Joyce left the public house and walked briskly away, but no-one yet followed him out of the building.
"Where is this scarred man Holmes? Have we missed him?"
"No, we have not, Watson, he will be here presently. Would you wish to remain in such a bawdy place, prone to brawls at any moment, when you have such a fragile cargo with you?"
I took Holmes point and a few moments later a man appeared through the doors carrying the box. "That is our man Watson," said Holmes. The man looked around before wrapping the box in a blanket he produced from under his coat, and then walking off in to the night.

Chapter 24

We followed the man on foot for several streets before he entered a building, not dissimilar to where we had found Mr. Joyce. He disappeared inside but we were not on him quickly enough to see in to which flat he had gone. Holmes took his glass from his pocket and crouched down towards the floor, following some lead which was unseen to my eyes at least. "What are you looking for Holmes?"

"I am trying to identify a trail from the man's shoes, the mud and dirt around that pub are quite distinctive since they are contaminated with dust from the ships being discharged in the port. I carried out an inspection of my boots last night when I removed them and discovered these strange particles in the tread which I had also found on the clothes I had purchased from the seamen."

"No doubt we can look forward to a monograph on the subject?" Holmes did not answer but continued his way along the corridor and up the stairs, stopping outside a door and standing up to put away his glass.

"Here we are again Watson, do you have your revolver to hand? I believe there is a strong chance you shall need it this time." For the second time that evening we stood outside a door with my gun ready and Holmes preparing to barge the door open. As he readied himself to throw his weight against the door we were taken aback when the door opened and the scarred man faced us head on for a brief second before his instinct propelled him forward on to Holmes and they fell to the floor in a fit of noise and limbs. I tried frantically to aim my gun at the attacker but the fight was a furious one and it was impossible to keep my aim on my target. In one deft movement, Holmes employed one of the many techniques he had learnt from his visits to his oriental parlours and the scarred man fell back against the wall, winded only for a second. He ran back inside the flat as Holmes and I gave chase in to the dimly lit rooms.

We rounded on the man as he grabbed the box which we had seen constructed only a short time ago, "Get back or I'll kill you, this is filled to the brim with gunpowder and I'll take you with me." His eyes blazed at us, and there was a fierce snarl set on his mouth, "who are you and what do you want with me?"
I kept my revolver trained on him and it was Holmes that answered, "We know what you have been about, and we also know that you are holding a very dangerous item and we shall keep our distance."
"Tell your friend to put his gun away, things like that have a habit of going off unexpected. Throw it over here now." I did as he asked, but I was not unduly perturbed since I would fear taking a shot at the man would simply wound him and he would set off the explosion in any event. "Now, who are you…"
"My name is Sherlock Holmes." The man almost laughed,
"You are Sherlock Holmes? Well, well that is unexpected, that you should come to me instead of the other way around. I presume your accomplice here is known as Watson?"
"This is Doctor Watson, yes" Holmes replied. "I see you have the advantage over us."
"Oh, I have more than that Mr. Holmes, much more than that. It's a funny thing how it works out sometimes, but I was going to be seeing you tomorrow, sort of a present for you."

He lifted the box, "but you've gone and spoiled the surprise now." The snarl on his mouth turned to a twisted grin, "well this is a bit more difficult now isn't it?"
"It would seem so," said Holmes, "how do you propose we resolve matters?"
"Well that's a question that requires some thought, but I suppose we can just wait here while I ponder it? You're in no hurry I presume?" He laughed at his remark, as if we had any choice but to accept his suggestion but Holmes was clearly unperturbed,
"No hurry at all, please take your time. The longer we are here the more easily the police will find us. You were the one who sent the bomb in to the Turners house I presume?" He eyed Holmes warily but the self satisfied rictus of his grin did not alter,
"I suppose it doesn't make any difference now, does it? That's right, I sent him the package. I saw you both go in to the house not long after it, although I didn't know then who you were. It is a pity that it did not take you with it now that I know who you are, it would have saved me a job." Holmes let out a small chuckle,
"That is true, but what is more is that it is a pity that it did not even take your intended target when it went off." I saw the man's grin falter slightly, "Mr Turner is in fact alive and well." The man laughed nervously,
"You're trying to meddle with me Mr. Holmes, there's no way that he could survive one of these. These are packed full of explosive, and I saw the smoke and heard the noise from halfway up the street. No, sir, you are trying to…"
"I can assure you it is quite true," Holmes interjected sharply, "Although Mr. Turner set the bomb off it has one very

obvious and conspicuous flaw which allowed him to escape with only minor injuries. I can assure you after that he was very much willing to talk to us about the scheme you all had going, not to mention your particular part in it." The man had lost his grin and his face had returned to a snarl,
"No, I don't believe a word of it...." He edged forward towards us, his anger growing and I could see in his face that he would rather be rid of us altogether now, "there's nothing wrong with this," he held the box up defiantly again towards us, "you don't know anything about these."
"That is where you are quite wrong, I presume you mean that we should not have met Mr. Joyce? A very informative gentleman I can assure you and again a wealth of information." The man again edged towards us, but his hand moved on to the handle on front of the box, his body shaking with rage. Holmes continued, "Both are with our colleagues in the police now appraising them of all they know. I am quite sure Detective Fowler will be on his way here with some of his constables as we speak.
"Oh I see, Fowler is it, then I should be most concerned," with that he laughed, "you really have no idea do you?" If Holmes were surprised by the remark then he gave nothing away to this foul man in front of us,
"I think you will find we know more than you believe. I have seen you several times now during the course of my time here and I knew instinctively that you were not the only person behind this escapade."
"Is that right, and why would you think that?"
"Clearly this takes no small measure of intelligence and brains and you, sir, would appear to have neither. You would seem to me to be someone with no aptitude for a life in the

criminal fraternity, in fact I can only assume that you have been rejected from their ranks already…" The man now took two involuntary steps forward, seemingly forgetting that his hands were occupied holding the box, but nonetheless wishing to take a lunge towards Holmes, such was his anger. As he did so, Holmes lightening reactions caught us all off guard, "Now Watson!" he yelled as he sprung from his position and clamped his hands on either side of the box, trapping the scarred mans hands on to the article. Once I had gathered my senses, which took only a fraction of a second but seemed like an eternity, I pounced towards the man, grabbing my revolver from the floor and bringing it down squarely on the back of his head. He gave a loud groan, as if the very noise had been knocked out of his head by my blow, and then crumpled to the floor. Holmes followed him down, hands still clasped over the box until it was clear our assailant was unconscious and the bomb could be safely removed from his hands.

"Well done Holmes," said I, my breathing heightened by the excitement, "very well done. What shall we do with him now?" Holmes placed the dangerous package on to a small table,

"Tear up that blanket there Watson and bind his hands and feet securely, we shall take him to the police in due time. But first we must try to find out what we can about our friend here, I wish to know the identity of our scarred man." I went to work ripping up strips of material and bound both hands and feet independently and then drawing them together to make it impossible for him to escape. What little furniture there was in the lodging Holmes hands quickly raced around, picking up any item to try to gain some clue to our prisoners' identity. Papers which were scattered on the floor next to the bed were scooped up rifled through before being tossed back down again with a dismissive gesture. I looked around in the other room, the smell from rotten food and other waste hanging heavy in the air but in amongst what seemed to be a random selection of cuttings from the newspapers I came across a letter. It was written in a tidy hand, and described some manner by which money was to be paid to our man and how in due time Turner was to be despatched by the appropriate means agreed. The letter was at first of no help whatsoever in determining the identity of our man, addressed as it was only to 'Dear brother..' but as I came to the end of the page and to the signature, I stopped.

"Holmes," I shouted, "I think you may wish to see this."

Holmes appeared in the doorway and I handed him the letter, my face ashen as I began to contemplate the next move. Holmes quickly skimmed through the letter and, coming to the end, he shot me a quick glance before stuffing the letter into his pocket and turning back around.

"Come Watson, let us carry our prisoner down to the street and we must make haste to the police office, there is no time to lose!"

Chapter 25

Although the hour was now becoming late, the police office was no less peaceful for it with constables coming to and fro depositing prisoners and then returning back to the streets. I noted momentarily how young some of these constables looked but more than that how tired they all looked. I did not perceive Edinburgh to be a particularly dangerous or crime ridden city but in my experience, and I am sure Holmes would concur, where you have such imbalance between the wealthy and the poor these worlds will sometimes collide. This was not withstanding that the port in the city was teeming with sailors from foreign climes and when in port for only a short time it was almost inevitable that drunken brawls would break out if not over a woman then over a gambling debt or a point of honour.

Holmes and I dragged our prisoner in through the doors and laid him on the floor, the assembled company passing a curious glance but more than accustomed to this type of occurrence. By now he had awoken and for the last twenty minutes of our journey had been lying on the floor at our feet yelling to the high heavens all manner of profanity and exclaiming that we would pay for this act upon him. Now inside the police office his volume had not become any more reduced and this only seemed to encourage the other ne'er-do-wells gathered here to form a monstrous chorus of disapproval. We were about to look for a willing officer to assist us when the matter was taken from our hands by a booming voice approaching from a door to the back of the room that we were in, "What the blazes is the meaning of this, shut up the lot of you or you'll be in the cells without another word!" The man who appeared behind this bellow was heavy with a face as weathered as any I had ever seen including those in my platoon in the desert. How such a face should come to be roaming around in Edinburgh was clearly due to previous military campaigns since to my knowledge the weather in this fair city would take one and a hundred years to result in such a complexion. The man bore down on us, "What is happening here?" Holmes extended a hand to the man,

"I believe I have the pleasure in addressing Sergeant McAllister? I recognise you from the description given to me by Constable Morthouse, he was most vivid in his recollection of you." McAllister eyed Holmes warily,

"Who might you be?"

"My name is Sherlock Holmes, we are here on a matter of great urgency." Holmes pointed to the scarred man on the floor, "Tell me Sergeant, do you know this man?" McAllister leaned down, grabbing the mans head between his large hands and surveying his face carefully,

"He looks like someone I should recognise judging by that scar but no, I do not know him."

"He has been involved in the bombing of the Turner house in Heriot Row, I presume you have heard of the incident?" The sergeant nodded as Holmes continued, "his name as such is not known to us but if you would look at this letter from his lodgings I would direct you to the name signed at the foot of the page. I watched as his eyes scanned back and forth down the page before coming to the bottom and reaching the same point that had set Holmes and I off in such a rush,

"Fowler?" he said, "this can't be Detective Fowler surely?" The scarred man at our feet began to laugh hysterically,

"Ha, you know nothing you people! You'll be sorry for this, just wait until my brother hears of this, you'll all be dead men." McAllister aimed a boot in to the prisoner's body,
"Quiet, or I'll string you up right now," he bent over and grabbed the man by the neck and hoisted him in one swift movement to his feet, still securely bound. "So you're the brother of Detective Fowler are you, how did you come to end up on the wrong side of the tracks? Eh?" He shook the man who continued to laugh,
"You don't know anything" he shrieked again through his laughter, his manner becoming more hysterical. Despite his predicament he seemed to be in a state of manic deliriousness, "Just you wait….my brother….."
"Of course," Holmes ejaculated, "how could I have been so stupid. Sergeant, I believe what our friend is alluding to is that we shall not find any help in this matter with Detective Fowler, as he is the man we are seeking. It is Fowler himself who is the man behind these schemes." McAllister shook his head,
"But he has been with us for years, why would he stoop so low as to carry out a bombing on a respectable man like Turner?" Holmes shook his head as I too began to see what it was that he was trying to make us see.
"No," said Holmes, "you are not seeing the whole picture. It is clear to me that it was Fowler that must have been behind this business. Turner was a man who was easily turned, his lifestyle had to be maintained at any cost and it was seeing this that allowed Fowler to coerce him into his plan. It is a fallacy believed by all such men that to have money and to lose it is worse than never having it, the motto of a shell of a man. Once Fowler had him on the inside of the bank giving

information out as to their likely targets then Fowler had the contacts to act as enforcers for their little business. I will warrant that there are plenty of men in the public houses around the docks who would be willing to heave a fist for a Crown's drinking money." McAllister was aghast but the colour in his cheeks gave vent to his obvious furore,

"When I get a hold of him I'll murder him, using the guise of the police to carry out extortion and violence. I should have thought better of him. What do we do now? Personally I've a mind to take this gutter filth in to a cell and see what information we can coax out of him, if you take my meaning Mr Holmes."

"I fear it would take longer than we have and the man is clearly a gibbering wreck, what value could we place on anything he told us. However, I would suggest he is taken to a cell and held as he is clearly an accomplice in the affair." Holmes looked around at the people now assembled watching the commotion which had occurred, "I do not see Constable Morthouse here." I looked around the collection of faces and could not see him either, McAllister did likewise,

"He was here earlier," the Sergeant told us, "he was…" he stopped, "…oh good God, he was with Fowler." I started as I recalled Holmes instructions to the young man, "Holmes, you told Morthouse to come here and tell Fowler all that we knew." Holmes momentarily cursed himself and then regained his composure,

"I fear I have placed Morthouse in grave danger, we must examine what would be the next move from Fowler? Assuming he is trying to clear the trail of all evidence where would he go next?"

“Where else is left?” I asked, “he has already despatched Turner and he would be the only man who could tell us of the whole game. If Morthouse has told him what we know then I would suggest that the main people he must be rid of now would be ourselves and Morthouse.” Holmes face tensed,
“We must put our thinking caps on, we may not have much time. McAllister, I believe we may have been too hasty in dismissing your kind offer to, shall we say, question our prisoner. May I suggest you pursue that line of enquiry?” The Sergeant nodded, “Watson and I will try to find Morthouse and with any luck Fowler will be nearby. We shall send word to you if we are successful.”
Holmes and I stood shortly afterwards on the main thoroughfare and racked our brains to think where we could look, “What about Fowler’s home?” I offered.
“I don’t believe so, Watson, why go back there when there is clearly work still to be done. No, we must look at this from the detective’s point of view, where would he go to fulfil his wish to cover his trail?” I could not think, my mind blank, but it was Holmes as usual whose brain rose to the challenge before it, “Of course, come Watson, we must find a cab!” He ran down the street to hail a two wheeler which was some way further along the road,
“But where are we going, Holmes?” I shouted.
“Where else is there evidence to be destroyed? If we assume that Morthouse has spoken to him of the files he had uncovered in his father’s office then there is the possibility of more there to be found. If Morthouse has relayed our findings to him then that is where he will head for.”

Chapter 26

From the street outside the offices of Morthouse and Morthouse, we could see a faint light flickering in the window which confirmed Holmes' suspicion that this was indeed the destination for Morthouse and Fowler. It was possible, I proposed, that it could be another individual and while Holmes was happy to accept the premise the coincidence would be too convenient,

"We must hope Watson, that it is not Morthouse's brother as it would be unfortunate for an additional person to become embroiled in this sordid affair."

"Very true," I concurred.

The door from the street was unlocked as Holmes carefully turned the handle and opened it only so far as was necessary for us both to sidle through,

"We must be very quiet," he whispered to me, "I wish to make the top of the stairs where we shall bide our time and see the lay of the land inside."

I had some small urge to rush in to the room with my revolver drawn and confront the fellow but in my head I knew it may have disastrous consequences. As we mounted the stairs I could hear movement overhead and at the top we stood quietly, out of sight of the main office which was to our left through a small reception. We both seemed to be holding our breath in order to better hear what was being said which I shall relay as best as my memory will allow…

"Yes sir, the files were in this cabinet here." Morthouse offered. I could hear drawers being opened and files rifled through, Fowler grunting to himself as he did,

"But where are the rest?" he growled, "You said there were more."
"I can not be sure but if we are to look through the cabinets we may find some. They seem to be in a chaotic order in the drawers." I heard Fowler curse,
"My own fault," said he.
"Pardon sir?" Morthouse asked as I heard more files being taken from the drawers, the riffing of the pages within, and then tossed to the floor being clearly of no use,
"I mean presumably the files may have been tampered with, perhaps by your brother I assume." Fowler said. "I would doubt that my brother would have been through them, he has enough work on his own desk without looking through that of our father." Further noise ensued, more drawers being opened and closed, doors banging and the sound of paper being scattered,
"Your father was clearly not a man of particular habits, Morthouse, leaving his affairs in this mess. If I had known of further files I should have…." His voice trailed off and the noise stopped,
"You should have what sir?" Morthouse asked, a hesitation in his voice.
"Nothing, keep looking!" came the barked response.

I cast a glance towards Holmes who signalled for me to ready my revolver which I did gladly, as he seemed to ready himself to spring from our position. Before we did so, it was Morthouse voice I heard next,
"Perhaps we should look in the safe, detective?"
"Do you have the key?" came the reply.

"Indeed…." I heard a scurry of footsteps and a large door being opened, clearly a door to a connecting room or large cupboard,
"Then come on man," Fowler was shouting, "get the thing open!" A moment's pause then I heard Morthouse again,
"May I ask how you know to look in there sir?"

At this moment Holmes took off in a sprint from our position on the stairs as I followed quickly behind with Holmes crashing in to the office, the door careering back on its hinges and stopping with the splintering of the wood. On my entry to the room, I could see the floor was covered with papers, scattered all around and hanging from drawers as though a tornado had swept through the room. To my right Morthouse was standing, his face shocked at the sudden intrusion. Straight ahead, standing just inside the large cupboard which must house the safe to which they had referred, stood Fowler. His face had registered shock for only a second before his experience and training had put him in motion towards the large desk in the centre of the office. I turned to look as Holmes was also trying to lunge towards this and I immediately saw what it was they were both trying to reach. A parcel sat on the desk, wrapped in brown paper with some small bumps down the front, exactly the size of the box we had seen made earlier by Mr Joyce in his lodgings. I felt instinctively that Holmes would reach it first, his martial arts training and his wiry frame highly agile in such circumstances but to my dismay Fowler was closer and scooped the box from the desk just ahead of Holmes,
"Get back" he shouted, his nostrils flaring and eyes bulging red, "Get back or I will take you all with me, don't think I

won't" He ripped a hole in the front of the package exposing the handles beneath and clasped them firmly. Holmes regained his balance and took a step backward, "You," Fowler shouted in my direction, "get in here now and throw that pistol here." I did as he asked, taking several steps in to the room and tossed the gun on to the desk.

"Good evening detective Fowler," Holmes spoke calmly, his steely nerve holding firm, "I see you have the advantage over us again. Morthouse I trust you know that this is our prime suspect in the murder of Mr. Arthur Turner not to mention involved in blackmail and extortion?" Morthouse mouth moved with no sound as he processed this information,

"But that is not possible Mr. Holmes," he finally said, "Detective Fowler?" the question hung in the air as Fowler watched Holmes carefully,

"I am afraid so," Holmes continued, "we have just had a most enlightening chat with his brother."

"What do you know of my brother? You know nothing." Holmes laughed,

"Funny, those were his words exactly. But I know that you were extorting money from local businesses using Turner's inside information in the bank. You must have made quite a tidy sum, but I wonder what it was that started to unravel the arrangement?" A sneer appeared on Fowlers lips,

"Very well Mr Holmes, you seem so very well informed but it will do you no good. If you know as much as you say then I presume you will know what I am holding in my hands here?"

"I do, we were witness to the power of the device at Mr. Turners house. You propose to eliminate us in the same manner?"

“I do, and it shall be blamed on our young Constable Morthouse, I shall see to that you can rest assured. The three of you plotting away in this office when I came up and tried to apprehend you but with the surprise of it you must have accidentally set off the bomb and you all died at your own hands.” Morthouse moved forward a step but Fowler turned on him, “Keep back son, or you’ll get the same as…..” he stopped short but Holmes completed his sentence,

“your father?” he said, looking directly at Morthouse.

“What! What do you mean?” Morthouse demanded.

“I believe what Detective Fowler is trying to allude to is that your father did not die of accidental means but was killed by him, am I correct?” I thought I could see a small glimmer of regret on Fowlers face, not for the thought of his victim but more as if he had made a poor chess move which had been spotted by his opponent,

“Very well, Mr. Holmes, if you wish to hear it, yes that is it exactly.” I could see Morthouse’s face turning red but under the circumstances he thankfully remained where he was and did not try anything foolish, “I heard from my men on the street that some of our, what shall we say, customers, had been seen calling here. Clearly I could not allow that and the lawyer was just getting a little bit too inquisitive for my liking. It didn’t take too much to dispose of him, he was old and his breathing easily stopped by forcing some bread down his throat, making it seem like a tragic accident.” Fowler ran a hand along the desk in front of him, “he slumped down right here in front of my very eyes. Now,” he asked, “you tell me something Mr. Holmes, how did you know I was involved?”

"That part I am sad to say was quite by chance, your brother gave that away due to his delusional ramblings. It was then a case of putting two and two together and drawing the only conclusion possible. What led us here were the files as I knew that you would want to remove any further evidence, and the link to the explosion was also clearly evident."
"How so?" asked Fowler.
"On my arrival in Edinburgh I had read in the local newspaper of an explosion, thought to be a gas leak, which had killed one unfortunate victim, Charles Lamont. After what had happened to Mr. Turner and recalling the name of Lamont in the file Morthouse had acquired the connection between the two was quite plain." Fowler's sneer had returned,
"Very well done Mr Holmes, you shall make a detective yet."
"But if I may also ask one thing which puzzles me?" Fowler gestured for him to continue, clearly relishing the chance to demonstrate his prowess, "why did you dispose of Mr. Turner? Surely with that being done your route to the information you needed was no more?"
"That is true," replied Fowler almost forlornly, "but after the way in which he had despatched Woodbridge he had become too much of a liability, his nerve had gone."
"Aah yes, poor Mr. Woodbridge, poisoned with laudanum at the hand of Mr. Turner. I presume that he had insisted he take care of Woodbridge personally due to his affection for the man and then made quite a hash of the matter?" I felt Holmes matter of fact tone enquiring on the manner in which Woodbridge had been killed somewhat obtuse but his enquiry was met with a similar matter of fact response,

"Quite right, Woodbridge had become too close to the truth while working as Turners right hand man at the bank. I had warned him not to allow someone in too close but he was a fool to himself, I believe he had misguided paternal feelings to the boy. Despite a very lucrative offer he was not willing to be turned but to give him his due he was honourable enough to allow Turner time to confess and withdraw from our business rather than go straight to the police."

"Ironic that it was that very honour that you took advantage of to kill him," Holmes replied in a cold tone. "Come now Mr. Holmes, we must be realistic in such circumstances. Personally I would have taken him off and had him killed much more quickly but Turner, no, he wanted to do it in a more gentlemanly manner and poison him in his bed. After that we could arrange for the body to be removed and I would take care of the rest."

"But," Holmes interjected, "Turner proved to be incompetent even at that, giving too low a dose to Woodbridge to kill him? Clearly his knowledge was amateur at best."

"That was unfortunate and before he knew it Woodbridge had staggered from his room and had fallen down the stairs, the force of the blow to his head perhaps in league with the poison in his system killing him."

"But unfortunately in full view of the rest of the household?"

"Indeed, and in doing so it became impossible for me to cover things up. We played the game of blaming it on the supposed haunting…"

"By making the maid an unwilling accomplice?" Holmes interrupted.

"Yes, Turner had caught her one night but had told her to continue with it until he said otherwise, thinking it would be helpful to be rid of Woodbridge, but he did not seem to be frightened by the incidents. In any case, after that Turner wanted out and became convinced that he would be caught. I thought I had him under control until you showed up on the scene and he became even more convinced of the certainty of discovery."

"So you had no option but to dispose of first the maid, and then Turner to ensure the trail would not lead to you?" Fowler nodded quite casually which I found particularly chilling,

"I had to do as was necessary Mr Holmes. In that respect I had thought that I would be able to take care of my final problem with a little more subtlety than I will have to do now." He smiled and held forward the box in his hands, tilting it towards us to show the address written neatly on the top. I let out a gasp as I read Holmes name and the address for my cousin underneath,

"But you could have killed us all, my cousin and the children included!" I exclaimed, my horror turning to anger.

"Doctor Watson, there are always winners and losers in such matters and you are the final part of the trail which can lead to me, along with Mr. Holmes and young Morthouse here."

As Fowler had been revelling in the account of his deeds, unseen by him but spotted by me, Morthouse had been inching very slowly and carefully closer towards Fowler. I had deliberately not looked at him during the discussion with Holmes lest my gaze draw attention to the movement but he had been able to move within striking distance of Fowler.

Morthouse's face was set like stone, his eyes burning into Fowler, the rage he must be feeling inside for the murder of his father was clearly evident, his young age seeming to fade in to the anger of a man twice his years. Almost as if suddenly remembering Morthouse's presence to his left Fowler turned his head, the box still tilted in our direction. Morthouse let out a fierce roar as he lunged forward catching Fowler wrong footed, his hands grabbing for the box and gaining some purchase on it before Fowler was able to wrestle it back again and step back out of reach. Morthouse did not miss a beat as he grabbed my revolver from the desk and levelled it towards Fowler, pulling the trigger three times in quick succession.

Fowler jolted violently as the bullets pierced his torso, his hands instinctively releasing their hold on the deadly package as they clasped to his chest. The box fell to the floor and I tensed myself ready for the roar of the explosion but it did not come. The box landed on its front, preventing the small drawers from opening and setting the detonation in motion.

Morthouse stood over Fowler, the gun aiming directly at the stricken detectives head,

"You murdered my father," he hissed at the man, "you shall pay with your life now."

"Morthouse!" Holmes shouted, startling the young constable out of the intense focus he held on Fowler, "do not go down this path, it is one that is fraught with danger and regret."

"Mr. Holmes, I have had to mourn my father and now I find that his was not some unavoidable accident but the act of a cold and brutal murderer. If I do not take my revenge on this man now then what does that say about my love for my father?"

"If you take your revenge, what does it say about everything your father stood for?"

"What do you mean?" Morthouse asked.

"I mean he was a man of the law, he fought on the side of right and for justice all of his professional life. I do not feel that a man would dedicate himself to the application of the law for so many years and then condone you taking it in to your own hands, now would he?" Morthouse held steady for a moment before lowering the gun and stepping back,

"You are right. This is not the way, the law shall deal with him if he survives long enough to stand trial for his evil. But I shall not lower myself to his level." His shoulders slumped and his arms fell to his side, his grip on the gun loosening slightly, "Perhaps you would be good enough Mr. Holmes to fetch my colleagues who will take our prisoner in to custody?"

"Indeed, Watson perhaps you may assist me?" I nodded and walked out of the office door and Holmes followed after me, glad as I was to remove myself from the scene and have a chance to speak to Holmes on what we had just experienced. I was no more than two steps from the room when the report of my revolver cracked behind us and we instinctively turned, throwing ourselves against the wall in defensive posture.

The sight that greeted us was that of Morthouse standing over the now lifeless body of detective Fowler, the muzzle of the gun smoking faintly, a look of serene calm on the young constable's face, "Morthouse, what have you done?" I asked. Morthouse dropped the gun from his hand and moved away from the body,

"I had no choice," he said quietly, "as I was turning to move away his hand made for the bomb, he surely intended to pull the drawer and detonate the device. I had to stop him before he killed us all." I looked towards Holmes who was as always unperturbed by the situation in front of him,

"I am sure that would be the case," said Holmes, "our thanks for your quick actions Morthouse."
"Holmes….?" I asked,
"Fowler was the master of his own destiny Watson, as we all are, and so shall it always be."

Chapter 27

Our final day in Edinburgh was, compared to the events of the previous day, a seemingly lacklustre affair. Following the death of detective Fowler we were questioned long in to the night by the police during which time they pieced together the whole affair as primarily relayed to them by Holmes and Morthouse. My part in the terrible business being limited to the latter stages I had little to offer, but was more than able to support Morthouse in his story of the bloody conclusion to the events.

I slept until just after noon and, rising to find not only Holmes, but my cousin and his wife also, in the dining room partaking of lunch, I duly joined them despite my hunger being absent for the time being.
"I believe that your relaxing holiday to Edinburgh," Patrick mused, "has left you feeling more exhausted than before you came?"
"That may be true, however one thing we can not accuse it of is being uneventful. I trust that things are now resolved, Holmes?" He was as usual smoking his pipe and was sitting ponderously at one end of the table,
"I believe so, Watson. Following our testimony and with the backing of Sergeant McAllister, we have been exonerated, as well as our young friend Morthouse. There is the matter of some large amount of embarrassment not only to the bank but also to the police but that must be managed by others as best as possible," he blew out a long cloud of smoke as he paused. "My concern however is for Morthouse's future as he seems very much shaken by the revelation about his father…"

"As you would expect," said I, surprised that Holmes would expect otherwise.
"Yes, Watson, but more than that I see he has feelings of doubt and confusion about his future direction in life. His ambition was to join the police but he now finds that even there you have such men as Fowler." I was dismayed to hear this as I could see Morthouse had the makings of a fine policeman,
"I trust you convinced him that there may be a rotten apple in every barrel, Holmes, but once it is removed the remainder is sound?" Holmes said nothing for a moment, drawing deeply on his pipe,
"I tried Watson, but in my own experience there will always be another apple on the turn to take the place of the one since removed. Such is life my friend."
"Maybe so, but that would be a rather dim view of humanity if we should all look upon it thus, would it not?" Holmes rose from his chair suddenly,
"Watson, you are a marvel," he exclaimed, "you see the worst of human behaviour and yet you still see redemption."
"I shall take that as a compliment," said I, bringing the discussion to a close, "now, I may manage a spot of that lunch."

We all spoke fondly of our week in Edinburgh and I enjoyed this chance to discuss further with Patrick some of the medical matters which had arisen this week. Despite my decision to return to London, there was still some small part of me which yearned to take up the post and immerse myself in the medical world again, forgetting the crime and the

villains that my path with Holmes would no doubt take me in to contact.
We had planned to take a walk through the city as a prelude to our journey home but due to the late hour we had risen, and our prolonged conversation, we found ourselves in need of a hansom to take us to the station for the overnight train to London. Our bags were put on to the cab and we made our way outside,
"I will come with you to the station, John," Patrick offered.
"Really there is no need Patrick, I would not wish to take you away from your family, we are now readily acquainted with the city and will be fine under our own steam. But your offer is appreciated," I added quickly, not wishing to seem ungrateful.
"Remember you are more than welcome to return anytime, John, there will always be a place at our table for you if you should wish it, and for you Mr. Holmes of course." Holmes nodded and smiled graciously as did I but deep within me I knew that I should not return to Edinburgh, at least not for a long time. It had been a moving experience to come to know Patrick a little more but at the same time I did find solace now in Holmes earlier warning, to beware a kindred spirit as it may be a blessing or a curse. Patrick was family and for that I was very glad, but I must take the future in to my own hands and cut my own cloth accordingly. I supposed I now understood Morthouse's position in wishing to remove himself from underneath the control of his older brother, and to make his own mark in the world. For both of us we should be grateful for the support, but also ensure we did not come to rely on it as a crutch.

Our journey to the station was a silent one, which I must confess was more due to me this time than it was Holmes. The sights of Edinburgh went past us and I idly took them in until our arrival at Waverley station where I saw a familiar figure step forward to greet us,
"Constable Morthouse," said I, "I hope you are not here to meet us on official business?" He laughed slightly,
"No, Doctor Watson, not at all. I wished to offer my thanks to you and perhaps especially, if I may say, to you Mr. Holmes."
"My dear boy, you are most welcome," said Holmes cheerily, "I trust you are recovered from last nights ordeal?" Morthouse's brow furrowed,
"I have recovered from the shock of it, Mr. Holmes, but I must also come to terms with the revelations that came about as well. There is much to talk about with my brother and my mother as they have a right to know what transpired."
"That is something only you can decide," said Holmes, "but as you do, perhaps ask yourself what good may come of them knowing the truth? Perhaps they are better left to their blissful ignorance?"
"Perhaps, Mr. Holmes, perhaps. In any case, I shall wish you a pleasant journey. You must make your way to the train." He shook our hands warmly and I felt sorrow for his predicament, but in looking at him now, I did not see the young man that I had first encountered in Edinburgh. Before us now stood a man who had seen more of what the world had to offer, and had to bear the weight of it on his shoulders.

We made our way on to the train and settled in to our cabin, no different than the one in which we had arrived in

Edinburgh and I enjoyed the familiarity. We pulled off only a few minutes late and as I looked out of the window I saw Morthouse on the platform, offering us a single wave, before turning and walking back out on to the street. Holmes broke my train of thought,

"You are sure you do not regret your decision, Watson?" Holmes asked.

"No," I replied, "although a fine place, Edinburgh is not my home, and I am looking forward to be back in Baker Street and putting my feet up from my favourite chair. I trust that you found the trip worthwhile?" Holmes stared off out of the window,

"It was an interesting trip, Watson," he replied, his sharp eyes glancing towards me, "it shall certainly give you something to write up on the train journey home."

At this remark, I could only laugh heartily.

Also from MX Publishing

Four books on Sir Arthur Conan Doyle by Alistair Duncan including a an overview of all the stories (**Eliminate The Impossible**), a London guide (**Close to Holmes**), the winner of the Howlett Award 2011 (**The Norwood Author**) and the book on Undershaw (**An Entirely New Country).**

Short fiction collections from Tony Reynolds (**Lost Stories of Sherlock Holmes**), Gerard Kelly (**The Outstanding Mysteries of Sherlock Holmes**) and Bertram Fletcher Robinson (**Aside Arthur Conan Doyle**).

www.mxpublishing.com

Also From MX Publishing

A biography (**In Search of Dr Watson**), a travel guide (**Sherlock Holmes and Devon**), a novel where Sherlock Holmes battles The Phantom (**Rendezvous at The Populaire**), a novel featuring Dr.Watson (**Watson's Afghan Adventure**), a fantasy novel (**Shadowfall**) and an intriguing collection of papers from The Hound (**The Official Papers Into The Matter Known as The Hound of The Baskervilles**).

www.mxpublishing.com

Also From MX Publishing

Two 'Female Sherlock Holmes' novels (**The Sign of Fear** and **A Study In Crimson**) the definitive **A Chronology of Sir Arthur Conan Doyle**, a biography of **Bertram Fletcher Robinson**, reprint of the novel **Wheels of Anarchy** and the 4 'Lost Playlets of P.G.Wodehouse (**Bobbles and Plum**).

www.mxpublishing.com

Also From MX Publishing

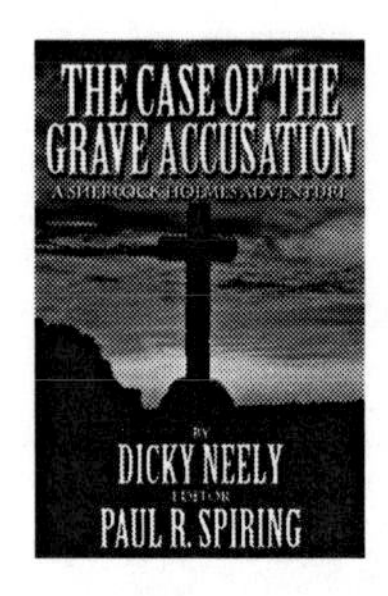

The Case of The Grave Accusation

The creator of Sherlock Holmes has been accused of murder. Only Holmes and Watson can stop the destruction of the Holmes legacy.

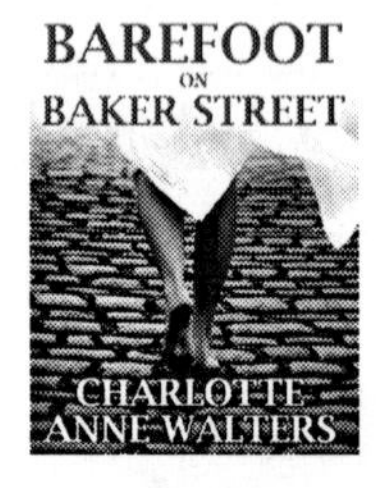

Barefoot on Baker Street

Epic novel of the life of a Victorian workhouse orphan featuring Sherlock Holmes and Moriarty.

Case of Witchcraft

A tale of witchcraft in the Northern Isles, in which long-concealed secrets are revealed -- including some that concern the Great Detective himself!

Also From MX Publishing

The Affair In Transylvania

Holmes and Watson tackle Dracula in deepest Transylvania in this stunning adaptation by film director Gerry O'Hara

The London of Sherlock Holmes

400 locations including GPS co-ordinates that enable Google Street view of the locations around London in all the Homes stories

I Will Find The Answer

Sequel to Rendezvous At The Populaire, Holmes and Watson tackle Dr.Jekyll.

www.mxpublishing.com

Also From MX Publishing

The Case of The Russian Chessboard

Short novel covering the dark world of Russian espionage sees Holmes and Watson on the world stage facing dark and complex enemies.

An Entirely New Country

Covers Arthur Conan Doyle's years at Undershaw where he wrote Hound of The Baskervilles. Foreword by Mark Gatiss (BBC's Sherlock).

Shadowblood

Sequel to Shadowfall, Holmes and Watson tackle blood magic, the vilest form of sorcery.

www.mxpublishing.com

Also From MX Publishing

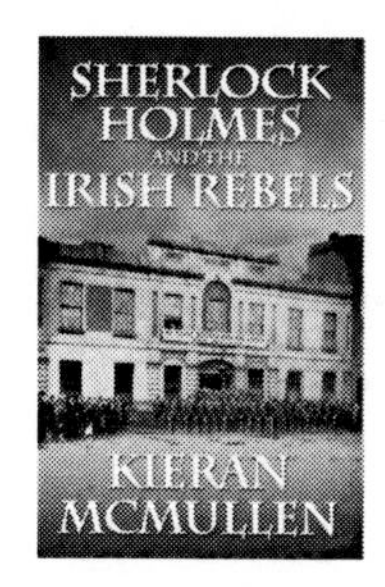

Sherlock Holmes and The Irish Rebels

It is early 1916 and the world is at war. Sherlock Holmes is well into his spy persona as Altamont.

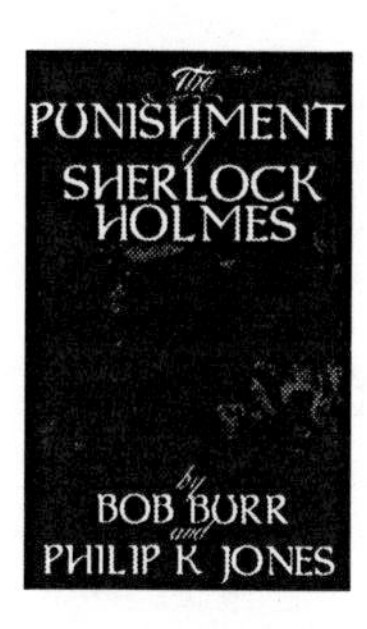

The Punishment of Sherlock Holmes

"deliberately and successfully funny"

The Sherlock Holmes Society of London

No Police Like Holmes

It's a Sherlock Holmes symposium, and murder is involved. The first case for Sebastian McCabe.

www.mxpublishing.com

Also From MX Publishing

In The Night, In The Dark

Winner of the Dracula Society Award – a collection of supernatural ghost stories from the editor of the Sherlock Holmes Society of London journal.

Sherlock Holmes and
The Lyme Regis Horror

Fully updated 2nd edition of this bestselling Holmes story set in Dorset.

My Dear Watson

Winner of the Suntory Mystery Award for fiction and translated from the original Japanese. Holmes greatest secret is revealed – Sherlock Holmes is a woman.

www.mxpublishing.com

Also From MX Publishing

Mark of The Baskerville Hound

100 years on and a New York policeman faces a similar terror to the great detective.

A Professor Reflects On Sherlock Holmes

A wonderful collection of essays and scripts and writings on Sherlock Holmes.

Sherlock Holmes On The Air

A collection of Sherlock Holmes radio scripts with detailed notes on Canonical references.

Also From MX Publishing

Sherlock Holmes Whos Who

All the characters from the entire canon catalogued and profiled.

Sherlock Holmes and The Lyme Regis Legacy

Sequel to the Lyme Regis Horror and Holmes and Watson are once again embroiled in murder in Dorset.

Sherlock Holmes and The Discarded Cigarette

London 1895. A well known author, a theoretical invention made real and the perfect crime.

www.mxpublishing.com

Also From MX Publishing

Sherlock Holmes and The Whitechapel Vampire

Jack The Ripper is a vampire, and Holmes refusal to believe it could lead to his downfall.

Tales From The Strangers Room

A collection of writings from more than 20 Sherlockians with author profits going to The Beacon Society.

The Secret Journal of Dr Watson

Holmes and Watson head to the newly formed Soviet Union to rescue the Romanovs.

www.mxpublishing.com

Also From MX Publishing

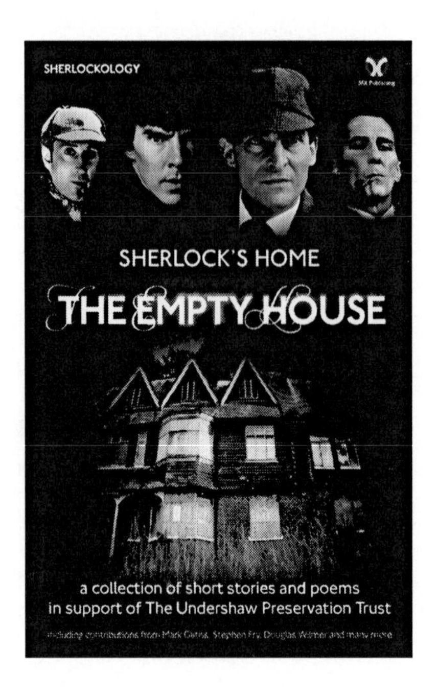

More than 40 stories and contributions from Holmes writers worldwide including Stephen Fry, Mark Gatiss, Nick Briggs and Douglas Wilmer.

Raising awareness for the campaign to preserve Sir Arthur Conan Doyle's home. All the royalties from the book go to the trust.

www.saveundershaw.com

Also From MX Publishing

A complete review of all the 56 short stories and the four novels in the Sherlock Holmes canon.

Taken from the astonishing blog Charlotte Walters wrote in the lead up to the launch of her debut novel Barefoot on Baker Street. Charlotte reviewed the 56 short stories one a day for 56 days in a row.

All the royalties from the book go to the Undershaw Preservation Trust.

Also From MX Publishing

America's first African American heavyweight boxing champion, Jack Johnson, has a chance encounter with a mysterious Irishman, named Altamont, when they meet at the boxer's restaurant, Café de Champion, in August 1912. Johnson's new relationship with the unusual man, with beady eyes and hawk-like nose, places him in an unusual circumstance to help Altamont get out of a tough situation.

Also From MX Publishing

When two prison guards are found beheaded in the barren countryside surrounding Her Majesty's Prison at Wormwood Scrubs, Inspector Lestrade seeks Holmes' singular powers to determine how the murders could have been committed in separate locations with the only footprints being those of the murdered guards themselves.

Also From MX Publishing

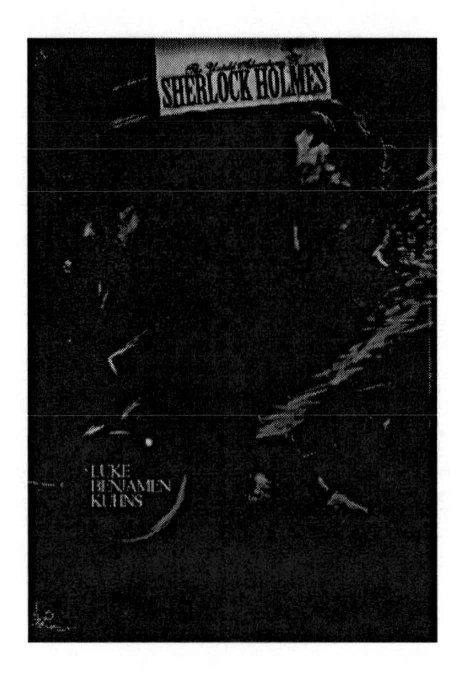

In the year 1933 an elderly Dr John Watson is looking back over his life and his time spent with his brilliant friend and master of deduction Sherlock Holmes. He writes in a letter to the reader that he has assembled a list of seven untold adventures that span from his and Sherlock's early years until the time of Sherlock's retirement. Watson explains that he wishes to leave, not only his family but the public with a final compilation of Adventures that he and Sherlock shared while he is still able.

www.mxpublishing.com

Lightning Source UK Ltd.
Milton Keynes UK
UKOW050609091112

201909UK00005B/23/P

9 781780 922829